MY DOG GETS A JOB

MY DOG: GETS A JOB

ELIZABETH FENSHAM

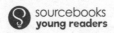

sourcebooks
young readers

In memoriam: Pippa Wilson and her dog, Ben.

-E.F.

For Monnie the collie: you chased sticks like a dog,
but you had the soul of a magical princess.

-J.L.

First published in the United States in 2019 by Sourcebooks
Copyright © 2017, 2019 by Elizabeth Fensham
Cover and interior artwork © 2019 by Sourcebooks
Cover and interior artwork by James Lancett

Published by Sourcebooks Young Readers, an imprint of Sourcebooks Kids
P.O. Box 4410, Naperville, Illinois 60567-4410
(630) 961-3900
sourcebookskids.com

Originally published as *My Dog Gets a Job* in 2017 in Australia by University of Queensland Press.

Library of Congress Cataloging-in-Publication data is on file with the publisher.

Source of Production: Berryville Graphics, Inc. Berryville, Virginia, USA
Date of Production: May 2019
Run Number: 5015026

Printed and bound in the United States of America.
BVG 10 9 8 7 6 5 4 3 2 1

1

My bossy big sister, Gretchen, calls it "fessing up." That's her way of meaning to "confess" or own up to something. She's always saying to me, "Out with it, Eric. Fess up!"

If my family calls me by my full name, Eric (instead of Eccle or Ec), I know I'm in trouble. Usually, it's about a crime my dog, Ugly, has committed—like leaving hairs on Gretchen's new bedroom carpet. She will storm out of her bedroom, holding up her eyebrow tweezers with a single, long, wiry dog hair dangling from it. She'll yell, "You and Ugly have invaded my room again! You're a sneaking little snooper. I'll make sure you're sorry if I catch you one more time."

These are nasty things for a nineteen-year-old sister to say to her nine-and-a-lot—almost ten—year-old brother. Apart from congratulating Gretchen on her clever alliteration (we're learning about this in school)—"sneaking" and "snooper"—I have decided not to answer back for two reasons. Firstly, I feel sorry for Gretchen because she broke up with Shane, her boyfriend. And secondly, she's right about me snooping.

I've had to look around in Gretchen's bedroom a few times when it's necessary to get some important information. But it's hurtful when Gretchen accuses Ugly and me of almost everything that goes wrong in her life. Still, I handle my sister much better nowadays.

UGLY'S
LITTLE
"GIFT"

I don't let Gretchen see me scared; it's rule number

2

one of the wild animal kingdom if you want to survive. Also, if I'm quick enough to say or do something funny like inspect her bedroom carpet with a pair of imaginary tweezers, then hold the "tweezers" up as if I've discovered something and say, "Well, look at that. I think it might be Gretchen snot!" Gretchen's rage usually fizzles out like a balloon that's lost its air.

While Gretchen says "fess up," my grandpa would say "getting something off your chest." Dad would tell you to "come clean." Mom calls it telling the truth. What it boils down to is that I really do have a confession. The first person I told was my teacher, Miss Jolly. She was cool. She said, "You're human, Eric. Lots of grown-up writers do that. The important thing is that you move on and keep trying."

BEING UGLY'S OWNER IS GREAT EXERCISE

3

2

I like the way Miss Jolly calls me a writer. She knows how I became one earlier this year; it was when I was feeling sad and angry, and I felt the whole world was against me—including my dog, Ugly.

I had really wanted Ugly (who was my eighth birthday present last year) to like me, but he didn't. I got all my bad feelings off my chest by writing about them. Just like Miss Jolly did with my first book, she says she will fix my spelling and other mistakes if I finish this one.

Apart from Ugly's name, which I'd given him because Gretchen had called him "as ugly as sin," I felt like I didn't have much of a say with my dog. When I turned nine at the beginning of this year, Ugly was more Mom's dog than mine.

Because I was hurt and jealous, one day I threw a gigantic fit. I did something that put me in danger. I wrote about all this in my first book, but I don't want to think too much about what I did. I'm ashamed.

Looking back, I can see that having a puppy in the house is kind of like having a baby who never wears diapers and who can already walk and chew. It can put a strain on the family. Everyone needs to be ready to do their part to help.

I had to learn quite a few lessons about looking after a dog. I'm much more grown-up now. I understand how I needed to feed, care, play with, and train Ugly before we could be friends.

Since I've opened up to Miss Jolly, I can come right out and admit how I'm disappointed with myself. Grandpa calls it a "sin of omission." This means it's about what I didn't do, but should have done. It's amazing how talking with another person about something that is getting you down makes it easier afterward to open up to other people.

My big secret is that in the book I wrote about getting Ugly to like me, I told the whole world I was going to write an amazing book for kids like me about understanding, training, and looking after your dog. I even had the different sections figured out:

- how to stop a dog from chasing a cat
- what to do if a dog poos under or on your bed
- how to stop a dog chewing your school projects or treasured possessions
- how to stop a puppy from biting your toes
- games dogs like to play
- reasons your dog stares at you
- how to tell if your dog is hypnotizing you and what to do about it

- ten smelly, yummy dog treat recipes
- how to stop a dog from eating other dogs' poo
- how to stop a dog from eating your socks or running off with your sister's tights
- what to feed a dog so it doesn't have stinky farts
- twelve reasons dogs have bad breath
- how to tell a dog's future by reading its paw
- tips on how to stick to training even when you don't seem to be getting anywhere
- dog psychology—how to tell if your dog is lonely, sad, embarrassed, jealous, angry, or bored
- useful and unusual tricks to teach your dog

But I haven't written a dog information book. I wrote one page and then shoved it in my desk drawer. It's embarrassing when people ask me if I've finished it.

"You've bitten off more than you can chew," Miss Jolly said.

I knew my teacher was using an idiom. We studied those at the start of this year. Considering I was going to write an information book about dogs, I thought Miss Jolly was choosing a great doggy idiom—you know, *biting* and *chewing*. What my teacher meant was that trying to write that kind of book is a little too hard for me at nine-and-a-lot years of age. Maybe I need to be double digits—ten—before I'm old enough.

I'm not a dog expert yet. Ugly still disobeys me sometimes. He can also be sneaky when no one is around. I mean, what is a boy supposed to do if his

UGLY THE
UNDERWEAR BANDIT

GRETCHEN'S
UNDERWEAR

dog is an underwear thief? Just yesterday, Ugly stole Gretchen's underpants again and tore them to bits and pieces. And I still struggle to stop Ugly from chasing Penelope (Mrs. Manchester's cat from next door). Penelope is such a tease. If I were a dog, I'd chase that cat to Timbuktu. (Grandpa says that's an ancient African city on the edge of the Sahara Desert.) And puppies that bite toes? I really don't know how to stop a puppy from doing that. I've even seen grown-ups squatting on their sofas so their puppies couldn't jump up at them. As for knowing why dogs eat other dogs' poo, I don't have a clue; it's a weird and disgusting thing to do.

3

Since my confession to Miss Jolly, it's been easier to start writing again. It's not the dog expert book, although I know I will eventually write it. Before I do, I'll take my teacher's advice and do some official research. I might even include some of what I learn about dogs in this book here. Mostly, I'm going to write about the kind and clever and a little bit naughty things Ugly does. After all, he is still a puppy—a very big puppy.

Ugly is a giant dog. We bought him from the dog shelter without knowing he'd grow to be enormous: huge paws, taller than me if he stands on his back legs, and a big head with sandy-blond fur flopping in his eyes. He has the same problem tall kids have—grown-ups expect you to behave better than shorter, younger-looking kids who are the same age.

Next to my friend, Hugh Cravenforth, who's tallest in the class, I'm now the second tallest boy. Grandpa was right when he predicted I'd grow into my big feet. I'm now a bit taller than Isaac van Rossen, who's the best in the class at basketball. One year ago, Isaac told me I'd never grow very tall because I was too chubby. He said my weight would hold me down. He was wrong. Anyway, thanks to having to walk and train Ugly, you can hardly tell I have a bit of a tummy. That Isaac! Big blue eyes. Hair as gold as butter. Top grades on all our tests. Miss Jolly thinks the sun shines out of him. She believes almost anything Isaac says. But she won't believe me when I'm telling the honest truth about my inventions project. (And, Miss Jolly, if this book is finished and you're reading it right now to check my spelling, I'm sorry to say that about Isaac. I think I might be a tiny bit jealous.)

Two Sunday afternoons ago, it was freezing cold as well as raining cats and dogs (as Grandpa says), so I decided to finish my "Inventions of the Twenty-First Century" poster in front of the family room heater. I spread the poster across the floor, then lay on my stomach coloring in a driverless car and adding labels to the other incredible inventions.

The next moment, Ugly had come back from playing in the backyard and was scratching at the kitchen door. I stood and walked to open it. Ugly didn't stop to say "thank you." He rushed past me, shaking himself so rainwater sprayed across the kitchen. Before I could stop him, he trotted into the family room where he walked straight over my poster, then lay on top of it. Once I managed to shift Ugly, I saw my poster was covered in giant, muddy paw prints and all scrunched up.

UGLY HAS NO APPRECIATION FOR SCIENCE!

On Monday morning at school, I tried to explain why I didn't have my project. Miss Jolly gave a fake yawn and said, "Please not another 'my dog ate my homework' excuse, Eric. Ever since the dawn of civilization, school children have used that one."

"It's not an excuse, Miss Jolly," I said. "Don't you remember? Ugly really did eat my matchstick model of the Parthenon. This time, his wet paws mushed up the writing on my inventions project."

"Do you know what the great Sir Winston Churchill said about that sort of catastrophe, Eric?"

I'd never heard about the great Sir Winston

Churchill, but I thought it best to keep the talking-to as short as possible.

"No, Miss Jolly. What did he say?"

"Churchill said, *Never ever, ever, ever, ever, ever, ever give up*. How might this apply to your inventions project?"

"Do it again?" I asked.

"Yes," said Miss Jolly.

"That's a lot of 'evers' this Churchill man used," I said. "Six!"

"Seven if you count the 'never'—because *never* means *not ever*," said Miss Jolly.

Grandpa says that Sir Winston Churchill was Britain's greatest prime minister. During the Second World War, this Churchill man kept everyone's spirits up when they felt scared and sad. I reckon my grandpa is just like Sir Winston Churchill. Grandpa often tells me "Never say die," which means the same as never give up. My grandpa is the best grandfather in the world because he's kept my spirits up many times. Sometimes he can sound a bit grumpy, but underneath the grump is a whole lot of kindness.

Anyway, I've taken Miss Jolly and Grandpa's advice like a man. I've started my inventions project all over again. I've also forgiven Ugly. He didn't mean to get me into trouble. Like I was saying, Ugly is still a youngster. You can never tell what he'll do next—for example, the vanishing chicken.

4

A few weeks back, Mom made the mistake of leaving a roast chicken on the kitchen table—fresh out of the oven. She wanted it to cool off, so we could have it with a salad for dinner. It was about six o'clock at night. All five of our Bright family (that's our name) were in the backyard. We were admiring Grandpa's new hen and duck coop. (As well as the healthy vegetables Grandpa grows in his vegetable garden, he wanted to buy some fowls, so the family can have fresh eggs too.)

After inspecting the coop with its neat, straw-lined nesting boxes, we strolled up the back steps into the kitchen. Lo and behold, no roast chicken. We looked in the oven again, just in case Mom had been forgetful. No chicken. We searched the whole house. Ugly trotted around with us. He was acting as if he was helping us to look. Although he was everyone's chief suspect (even mine), there was no evidence to connect Ugly with the theft of the roast chicken. Because the front door had been unlocked, we eventually decided the thief might not be Ugly; it might have been a stranger.

The next night, when we sat down as a family to watch a documentary on native South American animals, Mom went to rearrange a cushion on the sofa. She let out a loud "Aaaagh!" that sounded like a cavewoman going into battle with a wooden club. Underneath the cushion was a squishy, bony part of the roast chicken. Ugly had buried it. That's when he got into the most trouble he's ever been in.

Mom held that squished and smelly bit of chicken in front of Ugly's face, and everyone, including me, told him off about stealing our dinner. His tail was between his legs and his head was hanging low. He was so guilty, he couldn't look at us. Dad told me to put him out in the backyard.

"This hound was supposed to be well-trained!" said Dad. "If he's going to behave like this, he will have to live outside more of the time."

After an hour, there was a thunderstorm. Even though Ugly has his very own kennel with its fancy DOGHOUSE sign, I knew he was terrified of thunder and lightning. After I begged him, Dad finally said I could let Ugly into the house.

By the time Ugly slunk into the living room and lay down behind the sofa, the TV was turned off. We were sitting around doing different activities—Mom figuring out a crossword, and Dad paying bills on the computer. Gretchen was holding up a little mirror and plucking her eyebrows, so they looked like an upside-down smile. Grandpa was reading from a gardening book to anyone who'd listen about how to make magical garden fertilizer by filling a cow's horn with cow manure and burying it in the soil under a full moon.

I sat on the sofa next to Mom and started to finish my math homework. I'd only reached the second question when I noticed Ugly was now sitting right in front of me. He was looking straight at me. I ignored him, but he plonked a paw across my right arm so it was pushed down on my leg. That was the hand I was holding my pencil with. I pushed Ugly's paw off and started on my math sheet again. *Thwump*. Ugly's paw whacked my hand down again.

"No, boy!" I said. "Let me work."

Ugly looked deep into my eyes, opened his mouth wide, and said, "Whaaa oughhh whaaa."

I knew Ugly was trying to speak human. A few months ago, I taught him to say hello. Ever since, when he's been at home alone and our family comes back from an outing, he's so excited that sometimes he still

says "hello"—although it sounds more like "huuwoo." But this time, after the hidden chicken crime, I couldn't make out what Ugly was trying to say.

"You're in deep trouble, Ugly. I can't talk. I have to finish my work," I said in a very strict voice. I went back to my homework. *Thwump*. Ugly's paw slammed my arm down a third time. The pencil flew out of my hand across the carpet. I was about to get really cross, but when I looked at Ugly, he gave a sad whimper that sounded a lot like "oweee" or "sorry." I swear, two real tears came out of his eyes and rolled down his hairy cheeks.

"Ugly's crying, Mom!" I said. "He's saying sorry about the chicken."

Mom looked up from her crossword and leaned forward to look.

"They really do look like tears, Eccle," said Mom. "Everyone, come and look at poor Ugly."

Dad and Grandpa moved across to Ugly, but by the time they got to him, the tears had left only teeny-weeny damp spots on his face.

My sister, Gretchen—who hadn't budged from her chair because she was still perfecting her eyebrow arches—said in a bored voice, "Blocked tear ducts, more likely. Dogs don't feel emotions like we do, and I'm pretty sure they don't cry."

No matter what Gretchen says, I know Ugly feels

guilty, sad, and lonely when he gets into trouble—just like I do. And just like me, he often does something naughty because he's bored. I believe Ugly needs more challenges because he is a dog genius. When I told Grandpa, he said, "The Einstein of canines, eh?"

"You're a poet and didn't know it!" I answered back.

Grandpa and I laughed because he had cracked a joke and made a rhyme at the same time.

"So, what sort of challenge do you think you'll give the mutt?" Grandpa asked.

Without thinking, I blurted out, "Ugly needs a job."

5

Amazingly, a few days after the stolen chicken crime, Ugly found himself a job. Grandpa brought home three black hens and three white ducks. He locked them in their coop for three days to get them used to their home. After that, he let them out for a couple of hours before sunset. After school each day, Grandpa, Ugly, and I sat on the lawn watching the birds clucking, quacking, and pecking around the grass and under bushes, searching for worms and yummy insects.

The hens were like kids in the schoolyard. They'd hang out with one another from time to time, but then wander off to do their own thing. On the other hand, the ducks were like soldiers. I have no idea how they voted for their leader, but one of them was definitely the captain. Every time the ducks visited a different part of the garden, they would follow the leader in single file.

I had Ugly on a leash in case he was thinking "dinner" thoughts. It worried me that he seemed a little too interested in Grandpa's fowls. Ugly's ears were pricked straight up, and he was smiling so you could see his big, sharp teeth. His long tongue was hanging out of his mouth, and ropes of dog dribble were dangling down like those stalactite things that hang from the ceiling of caves. His tail was thumping the ground as if to say, "Now we're going to have some fun!"

"No, Ugly!" I said in a stern voice. "No!"

When it came time for the birds to be locked away, Grandpa opened the wire gate of their yard. I stood with Ugly to one side of the gate. In order to train him not to chase or bark, I patted his head, told him he was a good boy, and fed him treat after treat. The chickens squawked and flapped their way into their coop, while the ducks waddled in like really old people with bad hips. One by one they went in a neat, straight line.

I kept training Ugly (I call it chicken- and duck-proofing him) for a week. One afternoon soon after this, Ugly proved himself to be a star. Grandpa, Ugly, and I were doing shepherd duty once again. It was just after sunset. Grandpa opened the yard gate. We were about to encourage the chickens and ducks inside when we heard Mom let out a terrified scream from the direction of the kitchen. Grandpa and I raced up the back steps into the house.

Mom was standing on a chair, pointing at the floor. The biggest, blackest spider I've ever seen was angrily marching about on the floor. Grandpa grabbed an empty jar and shoved the opening over the top of the spider. He told me to bring him some newspaper. He used this to slide under the spider and trap it, then he flipped the jar upright. The hairy-legged spider was

trying to climb the glass walls of the jar, but Grandpa had it safely imprisoned.

For a tough old guy, Grandpa hates killing any living creature. Mom wanted him to spray insecticide into the jar, but I knew Grandpa wouldn't do that. Instead, he walked out the back door to the top step, took the newspaper cover off the jar, and shook the jar over the garden below. The lucky spider fell into some long grass.

"Good job, Grandpa," I said, patting him on the shoulder.

But Grandpa wasn't paying attention. He was staring wide-eyed at the garden. "Take a gander at that!" he said.

What I saw made my heart leap. In all the fuss about Mom and the spider, we had left Ugly on his own in the backyard. I had not finished chicken- or duck-proofing him, so what we were now looking at was amazing. Ugly was not chasing or eating our birds. Instead, he was quietly plodding behind the three ducks, still in single file, and herding them around and around the garden. Grandpa and I tiptoed down the steps and across the lawn to Ugly.

"Good dog, Ugly!" I said, patting him and fetching a treat for him from my pocket. "You're a sheepdog!"

"No," said Grandpa. "He's a duck dog."

From that day on, we let Ugly herd the ducks into their pen at sunset. He never tried to nip them. He never even barked at them. He just liked being in charge and making them march about.

One day, Ugly even saved the ducks' lives. I saw Mrs. Manchester's cat, Penelope, crouching like a ginger tiger in the grass on our side of the fence. She was staring with cold, green, hungry eyes at our flocks. Maybe I shouldn't have, but I said, "Penelope is over there, Ugly!"

One minute, Ugly had been sitting on the lawn beside me. Next, he was growling and bounding across to Penelope. She flipped over the fence like an Olympic high jump champion, then flattened herself like a pancake so she could squeeze under Mrs. Manchester's house. Ugly gave a last bark through the fence as if to say, "Don't you even think about hurting my birds," then he trotted back to me, smiling and panting.

"Good boy!" I said, patting him.

Grandpa and I were certain now that Ugly had a job, he would stay out of trouble. Life for Ugly was going along happily and smoothly. He was in charge of protecting the hens and ducks as well as helping to put them to bed each night. Grandpa said Ugly was "dedicated to his job." Everyone in the family, including Gretchen, was telling Ugly that he was the cleverest dog in the whole wide world. A few days after that, my family (especially Gretchen) changed their minds.

6

The way my family decided Ugly wasn't quite the cleverest dog in the world happened like this: I walked home after school last Monday. The front door was open. The hallway was as dark and quiet as a shadowy night, but that was pretty normal. Mom, Dad, and Gretchen were still at work. I could hear Grandpa snoring like an out-of-tune trumpet. He was having his afternoon nap on the sofa in the living room. What was not normal was that Ugly hadn't come rushing to meet me. I went down the hall. Second door on the left (opposite my bedroom) is Gretchen's bedroom.

Gretchen's bedroom door was a little bit open. Ugly

was sitting upright and as still as a statue at the entrance. Just like me, he'd grown into his huge paws. He was now a very big, shaggy dog who took up most of the doorway. When he saw me, he didn't jump up to say, "Welcome home!" He was staring straight ahead, ignoring me. His eyebrows were pulled together in a worried frown.

"Why don't you say hello, boy?" I asked.

Other than giving a little friendly thump of his tail on the floor, Ugly didn't move or speak.

"What on earth are you doing sitting in Gretchen's doorway?" I asked. "She's almost as mean to you as she is to me. No point in trying to be her friend."

Ugly sat there silently. I nudged him, but he wouldn't budge. He was like one of the queen's guards at Buckingham Palace. I

UGLY
THE
QUEEN'S
GUARD

30

had to give him a strong shove. I pushed Gretchen's bedroom door fully open and squeezed past Ugly inside.

Three ducks were huddling in the far corner. Slimy, smelly, green duck poo was on Gretchen's patchwork bed quilt, on her new carpet, and dripping down the walls. When the ducks saw me, they started quacking crankily.

"Oh no!" I cried. "I'm in for it!" I swung around to Ugly who was standing behind me. "What have you done?" I yelled.

Ugly put his tail down and looked at me with sad, brown eyes. At that moment, I knew he hadn't meant to be naughty. He had just become overexcited about his duck-dog job. He must have been herding them around the backyard. Somehow, the little army had marched up the side of the house and through the front door. That night, Gretchen wasn't as understanding as I had been. She behaved very badly. I won't repeat the horrible things she said to my dog and me.

On Tuesday, the quilt went off to the dry cleaners, a team of professional carpet cleaners came to shampoo the carpet, and I did my best to wash the walls. (There's a couple of little high up spots I couldn't reach that Gretchen hasn't spotted yet.) Despite all the hard work, Gretchen didn't have the manners to thank me. But I'm more grown-up now. I took her rudeness in stride.

Poor old Ugly has failed at his job—not from being lazy, but by trying too hard. Dad has been incredibly cranky about the cost of the quilt and carpet cleaning. He even muttered something about chaining Ugly up for part of each day and evening. "Keep him out of mischief," said Dad. "He can't be trusted inside or outside." Sent out back to the doghouse is one thing, but chained up like a prisoner?

This is the very first time I've ever thought Dad was truly wrong about something. I have good reasons. Firstly, Ugly can be trusted to play in the backyard without causing trouble. Secondly, it wasn't Ugly's fault the side gate and front door were open. Lastly, Ugly wants to be with humans. He gets lonely.

The only dog I've known to be tied up belonged to the family of a kid at school. I visited his place only once, but I never wanted to go back. Their dog was chained up to a long wire, so he could run up and down the backyard. None of the family went near the dog because it would jump at you and try to bite. I didn't have to be a dog expert to know the poor dog was being driven nuts.

"The duck disaster was not Ugly's fault, Dad," I said. "And anyway, you'll make him upset if you tie him up."

"Well, he's driving us up the wall. It's been almost two years of these shenanigans. I've had it up to here!" said Dad, holding his hand under his chin.

I'm afraid I lost my temper. "You want to torture my dog! You're a terrible, cruel, evil man. If I were a policeman, I'd send you to jail."

"Take those words back right now," said Dad.

"Okay, I take them back," I said. "If I were a policeman, I'd chain you up too."

I was sent to my room. I was supposed to think about my rudeness and be sorry. Instead, I thought about how to stop Dad even thinking about tying Ugly up. I spent the night trying to figure out what might keep Ugly out of trouble.

Like I've said before, Ugly is a dog genius. All geniuses love thinking up new ideas. They also need new skills to learn, or they get bored. Albert Einstein was a genius. Grandpa and I once watched a film about Einstein on TV. He had wild, sticking-out hair like Ugly. I bet when Einstein was young, he did a bunch of cool, wonderful things. His parents would have been totally exhausted from running around keeping him safe. It's exactly the same with Ugly. If we stay patient with Ugly, one day he might be as famous as Einstein.

7

By Wednesday, I needed to tell my friends about the ducks in the bedroom disaster and how Dad was getting difficult about Ugly. I was going to ask them what kind of job Ugly could do to keep him out of trouble. I knew one of my two best friends, my ex-fiancée Millicent Dunn, would have good ideas, so at lunchtime I went looking for her first.

Milly was down the back of the playground catching salamanders with Isaac van Rossen. I first recognized her by her brown ponytail and the blue ribbon she always ties it up with. She was squatting down, holding an open cardboard box while Isaac was using his hands to steer a salamander into it. She didn't even look up when I said, "Hey, Milly, I'm calling an extraordinary general meeting for ten minutes before the end of lunch." Milly was concentrating really hard on her salamander capturing.

"What's going to be extraordinary about it?" she eventually asked, her eyes still fixed on the salamander.

"Extraordinary" is a word Dad uses about some meetings at his work, but I'd never asked why. Just when I was about to admit I didn't know, it came to me what "extra" and "ordinary" might mean when they are put together, so I said, "They're special meetings where you talk about something that's usually ordinary but is now very important."

"Block him off with your foot!" cried Milly to Isaac.

I could see Milly wouldn't really listen to me until the salamander was captured, but the tiny lizard darted to safety under some leaves.

"He's escaped," said Isaac. "Sorry, Milly."

"No worries. We'll try again tomorrow," said Milly. Isaac wandered off to play Tarzan on the monkey bars. Milly stood, brushing dirt and twigs off her knees. "So, Ec," she said. "What's important about the meeting?"

"It's about Ugly. He's been getting into trouble 'cause he's bored. We need to find him a job, or Dad says he might have to be chained up next to the kennel we built for him. Condemned to the doghouse. It will be like going back into the orphanage for him."

"Let's ask Poppy Giles-Kaye, Alderney Stebbing, and Ruby Pinkster to join the meeting. They know lots about animals," said Milly.

Milly and I went looking for Poppy, Alderney, and Ruby. We asked Miss Jolly, who was on playground duty.

"They're playing their favorite game about wild animals; the one they've been playing on and off since

37

the start of the year," said Miss Jolly. "You'll find them with Barnaby Fitzpatrick under the pepper tree."

● ● ●

Barnaby is the boy who joined our class early this year—fair hair, large green eyes, and different. A few days before he arrived, Miss Jolly told us we'd have a talented new kid who has some difficulties that we needed to know about. On his first day, he was going to show us a storybook he'd written about himself called *Amazing Me*. Miss Jolly got us to write our own *Amazing Me* stories to share so that Barnaby could get to know us too.

Sure enough, one morning when we got to class, there was the new kid and his pretty, smiling mother sitting near Miss Jolly's desk. He had a big book on his knee. After Miss Jolly introduced them, we had to hold up and read our *Amazing Me* books aloud. We thought we knew each other, but we learned tons of interesting stuff we didn't have a clue about.

"We're all so different, aren't we?" said Miss Jolly. "Different experiences, interests, and different ways of looking at life. Now it's Barnaby's turn to show us his book."

Up until now, Barnaby hadn't said a word. He opened his book, holding it so we could all see. His drawings were amazing. There was writing under some of them. As Barnaby turned the pages, we learned he has a tree house in his backyard, he likes reading science and animal books, he has a four-year-old sister named Felicity, his favorite color is blue, he hates pizza but loves grilled cheese, he takes piano and gymnastics lessons, he likes the beach, he's a fast runner, he's a computer geek, and his favorite subject is art (no surprise there).

Next, Barnaby had drawn himself in a room with bright lights and lots of people with their mouths open. His hands were over his ears, and he wore dark glasses. You could tell he hates noise, too much talking, and bright lights. On the page, someone was speaking to him, but he was looking away. Underneath, he'd written, "I might not look at you, but I'm listening." On the next page, he'd drawn himself with a half-undone zipper across his mouth. Underneath, he'd written, "When I'm away from home, I find it hard to speak more than one word at a time. I go to a speech pathologist who is helping me talk." On the second to last page, he had drawn a long line like a highway going into the distance. He was standing about two-thirds of the way from the end of the line. He had written, "I am on the autism spectrum. My brain figures out what I see and hear differently than most people. Sometimes I don't understand what people are feeling. A lot of people are on the spectrum, but most of them speak." On the last page, he was looking happy and having a running race with some friendly children. Underneath were the words: "My family lives too far from a special school, so I'm trying this school. Miss Jolly will use picture cards to explain what is happening each day. I can use cards to tell her things too. I will also have a teacher's aide."

My best friend Hugh Cravenforth started clapping, and we all joined in. Barnaby flapped his hands and smiled. After that, we were allowed to ask Mrs. Fitzpatrick questions. Then Miss Jolly put up a poster on the wall that says: "Treat others as you would like to be treated."

Since then, Barnaby has made some good friends. On the day of our meeting about Ugly, Miss Jolly was right about Milly and I finding Poppy, Alderney, Ruby, and Barnaby playing the wild animal game together. Poppy was being a meerkat. Her hands were held neatly together against her chest as if she was begging. She was twitching her head from side to side. Nearby, Alderney was being a giraffe, gliding in slow motion. She was stretching her neck as high as she could to nibble at the dangling pepper tree leaves. Ruby was

being a rabbit, hopping all over the place. Barnaby Fitzpatrick was lying facedown on the ground. He was not moving one centimeter.

I leaned down and asked, "What animal are you being, Barnaby?"

It was like he was playing "dead fish." Not a muscle twitched.

"What is Barnaby being, Poppy?" asked Milly.

Poppy was still being a meerkat, so she wouldn't

answer. Just when I was getting a bit fed up, Alderney the giraffe said, "Barnaby's being a sloth."

"What's a sloth?" I asked.

"A sloth is slothful," said the giraffe, gliding toward another tree branch.

"They're the slowest, sleepiest animal in the world. They sleep hanging from trees for most of the day," said Ruby in a mouse squeak.

Poppy, the meerkat, at last decided to speak. "It takes them a whole sixty seconds to move six feet."

I crouched down next to Barnaby and said, "Hey, Barnaby, you're a great sloth! But you probably won't like coming to my extraordinary meeting because it will be all talking."

Barnaby broke the sloth rule. He turned his head to one side and grinned at me, then he went back to being a sloth.

"Poppy, Alderney, and Ruby, are you coming to Ec's extraordinary meeting? It's about his dog, Ugly," said Milly.

Poppy was one of the kids who helped with the survey I did earlier this year on how to get a dog to like you. Her idea about giving a dog a treat to make it like you was very sensible.

"We have to find Ugly a job," I said. "It's an emergency. Please, would you come?"

The three girls said they would like to come, but they promised Miss Jolly they would be Barnaby's buddies at lunchtime. Some of us take turns being buddies with Barnaby during our breaks. The teacher's aide or Miss Jolly keep an eye on him too. Barnaby can be fun to play with, but sometimes he can go ballistic. He might yell and throw things. Other times, he wanders off, and the teachers have to look for him. We understood why Barnaby's buddies couldn't come to my meeting.

Milly and I headed toward the back of the oval where Hugh Cravenforth was building a cubby with Liam Smith and Jimmy Brown. We had to wait until

Hugh finished balancing a bit of bark on top of a frame of skinny sticks before we could invite him and the other two builders to the meeting. Liam and Jack wanted to spend the last bit of lunch break kicking a soccer ball, but Hugh agreed to join us.

● ● ●

The three of us held our meeting inside Hugh's new cubby. We had to crawl in carefully and sit very still because the cubby was low and wobbly. I got the meeting started.

I said, "Welcome, everybody. Thanks for attending. You might be wondering why I've gathered you here together today." (I once heard Grandpa use those words when he had a neighborhood meeting at our place. It was about problems with the township garbage removal.)

"No, we are not wondering why you've gathered us together," said Milly.

"You've already told us about Ugly needing a job," said Hugh.

"That's how a meeting should start," I explained. "My grandpa does it that way."

"Okay," said Milly. She smiled in her friendly way. I could see the gap between her front teeth. "Do you want our ideas?"

"Yes, please," I said.

"How about another survey? Like we did last time when you wanted to know how to make Ugly your friend," said Milly.

"Good thinking," said Hugh, nodding his dark, curly head.

"Lots of ideas are better than three people's," said Milly.

I wasn't that sure about experimenting again on Ugly with tons of kids' ideas. He had a pretty confusing time when I tried out my friends' suggestions on him. I got into deep trouble when I tried Miles Bucknell's idea about giving him a bone; I shouldn't have hacked off part of the leg from Mom's expensive lamb roast. And Alara Güleçoglu-Park's idea about hypnotizing Ugly might have sounded brilliant, but Grandpa didn't appreciate me using his antique pocket watch to swing in front of Ugly's big brown eyes. Besides, Ugly has a bit of an attention problem. He wasn't concentrating on the swinging watch. He just wanted to eat it.

"Maybe your ideas will be enough," I said.

"Come on, Ec," said Milly. "Ideas from four people really aren't enough! I'll organize the survey."

The next day, four days after the duck disaster, was Thursday. Milly arrived at school with the survey typed up. It said:

"Eric's dog, Ugly, needs a job to keep him from doing naughty things. Please write down an idea on this sheet for a job a dog can do."

We passed the survey around at recess. Quite a few kids in grade school wanted to help with the survey. Here's some of their best ideas:

Sarah Gloor. *Grade Five. Eleven years old:*

"Personal trainer."

Eden Hogg. *Grade Five. Eleven years old:*

"A tour guide in the snowy mountains—like a St. Bernard dog."

Max Smith. *Grade Three. Eight years old:*

"A soccer coach—teach the kids to chase the ball."

Liam Smith. *Grade Four. Ten years old:*

"A dog trainer—a dog who trains dogs."

Oli Barlass. *Grade Six. Twelve years old:*

"A baby warmer for cold winter nights."

Jemima Brown. *Grade Five. Eleven years old:*

"Sheepherder—shepherd dog."

Lucy Blogg. *Grade Six. Twelve years old:*

"Eco-friendly vacuum cleaner."

Gennie Wilson. *Grade Five. Eleven years old:*

"Alternative energy—most powerful gas on earth, or a guard and sniffer dog."

Ben Segala. *Grade Five. Ten years old:*

"A dog rescuer—a dog who rescues dogs."

Angus Fletcher. *Grade One. Seven years old:*

"A gold and diamond miner or searcher for dinosaur bones."

Skye Denbigh. *Grade One. Seven years old:*

"Post office stamp licker."

Miles Bucknell. *Grade One. Seven years old:*

"A shaggy dog washer."

Emily Wright. *Grade One. Seven years old:*

"A Seeing Eye dog."

Merri Spalding. *Grade Two. Eight years old:*

"A rabbit chaser and veggie garden protector."

Ruby Pinkster. *Grade Four. Ten years old:*

"An empty plate licker at a restaurant."

Tilly de Lacy. *Grade Five. Eleven years old:*

"A penguin protector—like in the true story about penguins on the island."

At lunchtime, Milly, Hugh, and I had a second extraordinary meeting squashed into Hugh's cubby.

"The next step is to choose the most doable ideas,"

said Milly. "For example, we live hours and hours from places that have snow in winter, so Ugly has no chance of rescuing people lost in the snow."

"Although Oli Barlass's idea is good. Ugly makes a good hot-dog-water bottle in winter," I said.

"What on earth?" asked Hugh.

"A doggish hot water bottle," I said. "Ugly is a warm, hairy friend to snuggle up to in freezing weather. Babies would love him."

"That's hardly a job," said Hugh. "And there's no mom I know who wants her baby to have a hot-dog water bottle."

We added this to other impossible or "too difficult" jobs such as a miner, a shaggy dog washer, a circus dog, a sheep protector, a penguin protector (there's no circus, sheep, or penguins around here), a stamp licker (most people send emails now), a vacuum cleaner (Milly explained that dogs only eat food, not dirt and scrappy garbage), an alternative supply of gas (Hugh said to make this work, it would need squillions of dollars poured into scientific research), a Seeing Eye dog (the only person I know who has problems with seeing is Grandpa; I didn't think he would let Ugly lead him around. Besides, Grandpa has glasses), and a plate licker (very unhealthy).

In the end, our survey ideas shrank significantly. Hugh tried to make us get rid of dinosaur bone finding. He said it would be a waste of time because our area never had dinosaurs, but Hugh was wrong. Milly knows a lot about dinosaurs. She said that dinosaur remains have been found close to us. She told us the name of a dinosaur bone finder—it's a paleontologist. I know for sure that's the right way to spell it; I checked with Miss Jolly. This ginormous word is pronounced like: pail-ee-on-tol-ogist.

After we agreed to keep paleontologist on the list, Milly read out the leftover, doable jobs:

- personal trainer
- soccer coach

- dog trainer
- lost dog detective
- guard dog
- dinosaur bone finder
- rabbit chaser and veggie garden protector

"Maybe we ..." said Milly.

Those were the last words spoken at that meeting. Barnaby ran toward our cubby. He was screaming like he was being chased by a *Tyrannosaurus rex* (which he wasn't, of course, because dinosaurs are extinct). Miss Jolly was running, trying to catch up with him. As he ran past, he knocked off the roof, then the rest of the cubby collapsed around us. Once we had scrambled out, the three of us helped Miss Jolly look for Barnaby. We knew that something must have upset him badly. Maybe someone had teased him. When this happens, Barnaby is great at disappearing.

Just as the bell rang, we found Barnaby hiding

under a bush down near the school boundary fence. He wouldn't come out for Miss Jolly, so I crawled under the scratchy branches and leaves to sit with him. For a while, I didn't say anything. Barnaby likes to be quiet after he's been all shaken up.

When I thought Barnaby was ready, I started talking to him. Barnaby likes stories. I told him all about Ugly: how I'd gotten him for a birthday present, how my sister, Gretchen, reckoned he was ugly and so I had decided to call him that, and how I'd had to learn to look after Ugly and train him. Next, I told Barnaby about Ugly's duck job going wrong, and that my friends and I were trying to find a better job for him. Barnaby wasn't looking at me, but he was quiet in the sort of way that I knew he was carefully listening. I knew for sure he'd understood me when I said, "If you come with me up to our class-room, I'll show you a picture of Ugly that I keep in my school bag."

Right away, Barnaby scrambled out from under the bush. He tugged at my shirt as if to say, "Let's go."

Barnaby started walking fast toward the classroom, pulling me along with him. We made it there before Miss Jolly and my friends did.

The picture I kept in my bag was of Ugly on the day he passed his obedience test. He was also given a golden "dog hero" tag by Mrs. Manchester's family for saving her purse from a robber. It looks just like a bravery medal. If you look closely at his tag, it says:

UGLY
DOG HERO

Grandpa took the picture with his old-fashioned camera. In it, you can see the medal around Ugly's neck, glittering in the sun. He was sitting up, tall and proud, smiling at the camera.

I handed my precious photo to Barnaby.

"Ugwee!" he said. He snatched it and pressed his face against it. When I asked for it back, he wouldn't give it to me. I tried to take it, but when I did, Barnaby pulled away from me, still holding tightly to the picture of Ugly.

Rrriiippp.

I was left holding a piece of my picture of Ugly—a part of his hairy, whiskery snout and an eye. Barnaby still held the other piece. He looked surprised and shocked, but then he crumpled it up and jumped on it!

At first, I was too stunned to speak. There was no way to get another copy of this picture. It was gone for good. My heart was hammering so hard, I swear I could hear it. My hands were shaking. I became like a boiling-hot volcano. I lost it with Barnaby. "I've had it with you! You ruin everything for everyone!" I shouted. The volcano erupted, and I yelled, "My dog would never, ever like you!"

Barnaby stuck his fingers in his ears and howled. He threw himself down. He was thrashing around on the ground. It looked like he was having a fit. It was scary. Miss Jolly had to get the teacher's aide to sit near him until he was ready to walk to the school office for a drink. Later on, I heard his mom had come and driven him home.

Milly and Hugh heard what I'd shouted.

Milly said, "This all started because you were trying to be kind to Barnaby. Here's a clean tissue to wipe your tears and your nose. It's running."

Hugh said I'd been way too mean. "I'd be upset too. It's fair to be upset. Barnaby needs to learn the right way to treat people and their things. But hey, don't be cruel," said Hugh.

I felt bad about saying what I did to Barnaby. But are we supposed to let him do horribly mean things and just shrug? I think Barnaby needs to learn how to be a good friend.

9

Miss Jolly also told me I should never say cruel things to Barnaby—no matter what. But she understood how precious my picture of Ugly had been—and how shaken up I was about losing the picture and seeing Barnaby throw himself around like that.

"You've just watched Barnaby have a 'meltdown,'" said Miss Jolly. "Children with autism do this when they can't cope and can't explain their feelings. Barnaby got distressed by accidentally ripping your photo. When he saw your fury, he got more and more out of control." I nodded. I couldn't speak because I was trying to stop crying. Everything my teacher was saying made sense.

"But you can learn something from this," continued Miss Jolly. "Do you realize you lost control and had a small meltdown too?"

That was a shock. Me, behave like Barnaby? Miss Jolly patted me on the shoulder. "It might help you understand how horrible Barnaby is feeling when he's upset."

●●●

When the bell rang for afternoon class, Miss Jolly let me sit outside with Milly until my heart stopped pumping. Then I was able to control the little sobs that blurted out of me like hiccups.

"Keep your mind on our challenge, Ec," Milly said. "The picture is gone, but you still have Ugly. It would be much worse the other way around."

"You mean if Ugly were dead, but I still had my picture of him?" I asked.

Milly nodded. She was right. It was much better having a real, live dog.

"So take some deep breaths, and let's get down to business," said Milly. "We have to get Ugly a job. We will start with Sarah Gloor's personal trainer idea. I know a lot about it."

Milly really does know a lot about personal trainers. Her twenty-five-year-old cousin is one. Milly had so many interesting things to tell me that my tears dried up. She explained that when you are really, really out of shape and running out of breath when you walk up stairs, then people get a personal trainer. This is someone who is extremely fit and who makes you run and do exercises. Our idea was that the out-of-shape person would hold on to Ugly's leash and let him run so the person would have to run too.

● ● ●

On Friday, we chose Hugh as our business manager. He decided we needed to print flyers and pass them out to the neighbors around the streets. This is what we wrote:

UGLY'S
FITNESS
SERVICES

ARE YOU OUT OF SHAPE?

DO YOU LOSE YOUR
BREATH WHEN YOU ARE
WALKING UPHILL?

WE HAVE A SECRET
ANSWER TO YOUR
PROBLEMS!

EMAIL:
GET FIT @ DROPBY.COM
FOR A TOP-NOTCH SOLUTION!

OUR SUPER
PROFESSIONAL
BUSINESS
PROMOTION!

Ugly and I had a fun time delivering the flyers this weekend. The first one was to Mrs. Manchester's mailbox. She was sitting in the sun on her veranda, cuddling her cat, Penelope. Ugly looked really excited to see Penelope, so I had to hold on tight to his leash.

"What are you putting in my mailbox, Eccle?" she called out.

"It's a flyer for Ugly's next job," I called back.

"Ugly has a job?"

"He's a personal trainer. If you want to lose weight or get in shape, he will take you for a run."

"I'm a skinny old lady who gets my exercise with gardening and walking to the store, thank you. And my Penelope has had quite enough exercise trying to run away from Ugly!"

"I know," I said, "but you'd feel left out if you didn't get a flyer."

"How thoughtful of you, Eric," said Mrs. Manchester. "I hope Ugly is very successful with his new job. I'm forever grateful to him for saving my handbag and its precious contents. Oh, and by the way, thank you for the duck eggs you brought over yesterday. I'll use them to make a passion fruit sponge cake for your family."

"Yum," I said. "My favorite."

"And my good wishes for your flyers, young man. With everyone spending their lives inside, noses glued to computers, I'm sure you'll find plenty of out-of-shape customers."

"That's the plan, Mrs. Manchester," I said happily.

●●●

As I walked around the streets, I dreamed about what Ugly and I would do with his earnings. We'd make a "get fit" DVD. Ugly would become so famous, he'd end up on TV. When we got home, I went straight to the internet to see if anyone had signed up for some personal training. Gretchen was home from work, lying on the sofa reading a magazine. She got up and walked over to me, her magazine tucked under one arm, and leaned over my shoulder. "What are you so excited about?" she asked.

"Ugly and I are setting up a personal training business. I'm checking for customers."

"How are you going to do that?" Gretchen sneered. "You're hardly an Iron Man."

"I'm just Ugly's manager. He's the trainer," I explained. "The client gets to run with him." Then I got a brain wave. I showed Gretchen the flyer. "How about you get a free session, and we can use you for advertising?"

"But I'm not fat!" said Gretchen.

"But you *are* out of shape," I said.

Gretchen started making screechy-howling noises.

"Gretchen," I said, "you're sounding like an angry dog."

My sister then threw herself facedown on the sofa, bellowing into the cushion.

I stood there watching. It was fascinating. "Now you sound like an elephant with a nasty cold," I said.

Gretchen was in a bad mood all night. I should have taken that as a sign that Ugly and my personal training business was doomed. The only email I got back from our flyer was an angry letter. It was from a Mark Filipo who told me that I hadn't read his sign about "No Junk Mail." If I dared again to put any advertising material in Mr. Filipo's mailbox, he would complain to the township.

10

I thought Ugly's worst days were behind him. After all, Dad has stopped talking about tying Ugly up. But Ugly and I were in for another disappointment. Since I last wrote a week ago about the personal trainer flop, Milly and Hugh tried to cheer me up. They suggested we move onto Max Smith's idea: soccer coach!

Early this week, Hugh was allowed to come over to my place after school. He brought his soccer ball. Ugly loves kids. He said "huuwoo" and wanted to keep shaking hands with Hugh. When Hugh gave Ugly a hug, my dog cuddled up to him.

Hugh and I took Ugly to the park around the corner

to try out his soccer skills. Ugly ran for the ball all right, but when he caught it, he'd carry it away like a trophy. After a while, when Ugly pounced on the ball and sank his teeth into it, the trial was over. One dead soccer ball.

"Ugly doesn't seem to understand team spirit," said Hugh, looking sadly at his saggy rubber ball.

I thought the failed soccer experiment was a bad day. I was wrong. Last night, Ugly caused a disaster. Dad calls it a "catastrophe." Dad is right (although I think it is more like a "dogastrophe").

Up until about eight o'clock, it was an ordinary kind of weeknight: Ugly and me locking up the ducks and chick-ens, Dad

PFFT

helping Mom make a stir-fry, eating dinner at the kitchen table, Gretchen and me loading the dishwasher, some family TV, and then all five of us (six if you include Ugly) getting on with our evening's activities.

I was sitting on the sofa doing homework. Ugly was lying across my feet.

Dad was sorting business papers on a desk. He was picking them up, looking under them, then putting them down again.

"Where the heck is that USB stick?" he asked himself.

I noticed Ugly get interested in Dad's search. He plodded across to the desk. He had a friendly, helpful grin on his face. His ears were pricked up. It's as if he were thinking, "What exciting thing is happening here? Why is Father Bright shuffling paper around?"

At this moment, Dad tugged another bit of paper. Into the air flew a small, red USB stick. From where I sat on the sofa, I thought I saw Ugly catch it in his mouth. Caught out! If it was a baseball game, the crowd would be on their feet cheering. I heard a crunch. It seemed like Ugly swallowed the USB stick.

"Where did that stick go?" Dad asked.

When I explained, Dad started roaring, "Nooo! My work! My work!"

Mom, Grandpa, and Gretchen asked what had happened. I explained.

"Calm down," said Mom to Dad. "Your work will all be there on your computer."

"But it's not!" Dad cried. "It's too complicated to explain. Three months' work has gone into that dog's stomach!"

All of our family was now standing around Ugly. My poor dog was looking up at us with big, brown eyes. He slowly thumped his tail on the ground. It's as if he were saying, "I know I'm in trouble. Believe me when I say, I truly don't know what I've done wrong."

"I have to get that USB stick back or I'll be in trouble with my boss," Dad said.

"Give him some castor oil," said Gretchen. "Make him vomit up the USB stick or poo it out."

"No," said Mom. "We can't risk the USB stick getting stuck in Ugly's throat if he throws up."

"Besides," said Grandpa, "only Eccle is a witness. He might have only imagined he saw Ugly swallow the USB stick."

"We need to know for sure!" said Dad. He looked desperate.

"I have an idea," I said. "What about using Grandpa's old metal detector on Ugly's tummy?"

"Good thinking!" said Grandpa. He went out to his garden shed and came back with the detector in no time. I explained to Ugly what we were about to do. Then I rolled him gently onto his back. He looked like a confused sheep who was about to be sheared. I sat on the floor, holding Ugly's head in my lap. I stroked his whiskery face. "It's okay, boy," I said. "It will all be over soon."

Mom, Dad, and Gretchen kept the rest of Ugly still. Grandpa put on special headphones; if there were any metal in Ugly's stomach, he'd hear a *beep-beep* through them. Grandpa then turned on the detector's switch. He looked like a strange golfer. He was holding the long metal rod, guiding the round plate that was at the end of the rod over Ugly's hairy undersides.

The detector made no noise, so Ugly relaxed and enjoyed the attention we were giving him. He must have thought he was getting a very light tummy massage. After thirty seconds, Grandpa gave the thumbs-up sign. He turned off the detector's switch and removed the headphones.

"Eureka!" said Grandpa. "You can let Ugly go now!"

Dad cheered. We released Ugly. He jumped to his feet and shook himself. Then he headed for a private spot under the kitchen table.

I asked what "eureka" means. Grandpa said it's a Greek word for "found it." Grandpa supposed people still say "eureka" if they find something important they've been looking for.

So now everyone was sure where Dad's USB stick was. What now? Unfortunately, the next step was disgusting. Dad put me on poo duty. Starting from last night, for forty-eight hours I'm supposed to collect every bit of Ugly's poo—hard or squishy.

At first, I went on strike. Put a nine-and-a-lot-year-old kid on poo duty? Torture! No way. But Dad was in a very bad mood. "Man up!" he said. "That's my career in Ugly's stomach."

At that moment, I had a brain wave. I found an old sheet of Mom's and used scissors to cut it into large pieces. I then cut an apple-size hole in one of the pieces. I pushed and pulled Ugly's hairy tail through the hole. Next I wrapped the sheet under his back legs and tummy, up his sides, and ended by tying a big knot on his back. I had created the world's first dog diaper.

Sadly, Ugly didn't like his diaper. He bolted out of my

room. Next thing, I heard Grandpa shout from the living room, "What the heck have you done to the poor mutt?"

I walked into the living room to explain my dog-diaper idea to my family. Gretchen giggled in a mean way. By the time I had finished explaining, Ugly had rolled, scratched, and wriggled out of his diaper—and he'd knocked over a chair while doing it.

"Give me a break from this hound!" said Dad. "Ec, how long is it since Ugly has gone poo?"

"He did an enormous one when I took him for a walk straight after school this afternoon," I said.

"Okay," said Dad. "I badly need my space. Put Ugly out the back for a good, long while. Just in case, you can do a poo check when he comes in for bed."

● ● ●

It was dark, cold, and lonely in the backyard. As soon as I'd come inside, Ugly started howling. I wasn't allowed to go and comfort him.

"We've been too soft on that dog," said Dad. "He has to learn to enjoy his own company."

After a long half hour, Ugly went completely quiet. We kept him in the backyard until the hour was up. Then Grandpa got a flashlight and asked me to help check on him. Oh dear. We found Ugly angrily digging in the vegetable garden.

"My rhubarb!" cried Grandpa.

Ugly could not have picked on anything in the vegetable garden that was more precious to Grandpa. Grandpa and Grandma had loved their rhubarb. After she died and Grandpa had moved from their house to ours, he brought the rhubarb plant with him.

"Ugly's just upset," I tried to explain.

"Ugly's upset?" said Grandpa. "What do you think *I* am? Your father is right. This dog is trouble. He's a nuisance both inside and out of the house."

Grandpa left the flashlight with me. He stomped up the back steps into the house. I used the flashlight to check for any dog poo in the backyard. There wasn't any. I sat on the damp, dewy lawn, my arm around Ugly's shoulders.

"They'll be talking about you and me in there, boy," I said. "I don't want to scare you, but they might be discussing chaining you up. We have to be very clever. We have to get you a job that will use up your energy and keep you a bit quieter."

Ugly nudged my cheek with his wet nose. He leaned his big, warm body against me. It was if he was saying, "I'll be brave—as long as you are on my side."

11

To keep this sad and stinky part of my story short, for the last few days I've tried really, really hard to collect Ugly's droppings (that's what Grandpa calls them). No USB stick. It's one of the world's greatest unsolved mysteries.

In Dad's eyes, Ugly can't do anything right anymore. Ugly is now Dad's number one enemy. And Grandpa hasn't stopped being cranky with Ugly either. He's been calling him "that rhubarb wrecker."

One night, I was in my room getting ready to go to sleep. Part of my routine means organizing dear Ugly onto his dog bed next to my own bed. Just then, Mom paid us a visit.

"For heaven's sake, Ec," she whispered. "You have to keep Ugly busy, better exercised, and out of trouble—or else."

"Or what?" I asked.

"I hate to think," said Mom.

I couldn't get to sleep. There I was, leaning up against my pillow, writing away until late at night (like I am now) about my ginormous problems and worries. Ugly and I have enemies inside the house (Dad) and outside the house (Grandpa).

I was really counting on Milly and Hugh coming up with the perfect job for Ugly. They didn't let me down.

●●●

"Okay, we have to give this next idea from the survey our very best try," said Milly at our third extraordinary meeting held the next day at lunchtime under the pepper tree. "Ugly has eaten Mr. Bright's memory stick, and he's dug a hole and wrecked the rhubarb patch. Things are serious! It's time we tried Liam Smith's idea."

"What's that?" asked Hugh.

"Ugly is great at learning tricks and skills. He can teach other dogs."

"It's genius! Liam Smith is onto something here," said Hugh. "How can it go wrong?"

Milly and Hugh helped me create another flyer. Miss Jolly let me print out a bunch of copies on some scrap paper:

~ EXPERT ~
DOG
~ TRAINING ~
DOES YOUR DOG RUN AWAY
AND REFUSE TO COME BACK?
DOES HE NEED TO SIT AND
LIE DOWN ON COMMAND?
DO YOU WANT YOUR DOG TO
RESPECT YOU, THEIR OWNER?
~ WE CAN TRAIN YOUR DOG ~
IN ALL OBEDIENCE BASICS
~ WITH A WORD FIRST METHOD! ~
THE OBEDIENCE PROGRAM—
$10 A SESSION
CLASSES BEGIN THIS SATURDAY!
EMAIL —
ERIC 'N' UGLY @PELLMELL.COM

SUPER
PROFFESIONAL
BUSINESS
PROMOTION
~ 2.0! ~

When I got home from school with the pile of flyers in my bag, I suddenly realized I had another problem. Somehow I had to get Grandpa to say "yes" to helping with Ugly's dog training school. There would be no way Mom and Dad would let me go ahead without a grown-up keeping an eye on things.

I found Grandpa potting seedlings in his garden shed. I showed him the dog training flyer and begged him to help.

"Why should I agree?" asked Grandpa in a grumpy voice.

"Because deep down you like Ugly, even when he screws up," I said.

"You probably don't realize it," said Grandpa, "but I've already been doing an awful lot for that mutt."

"Like what?" I asked.

"Haven't you noticed that despite all the string of troubles like the USB stick and, before that, the ducks-in-the-bedroom drama, Ugly has not actually been chained up or put in an enclosure like your father has kept threatening? I've spent a lot of time trying to talk your father out of the idea."

"That doesn't make sense," I said. (What I didn't say, but wanted to say was, "Of course a dog is going to catch a USB stick and eat it if some fool throws it in the air. And as for the duck invasion, you fell asleep that afternoon and left the front door open. It wasn't Ugly's fault.")

What I *did* say to Grandpa was, "Why should Ugly be chained or locked up when I'm at school and everyone else is at work? It's only you at home during the day."

"Your father says that I shouldn't have to be responsible for Ugly when I'm at home on my own. I *do* have one metal hip from a fall, as you very well know. It took a long time for me to get over the operation. I'm even older now. I can't afford to have Ugly knock me over. And I won't put up with my vegetable garden being dug up. It's my pride and joy."

"I get that," I said. "But how come you've been standing up for Ugly when Dad is getting nasty?"

Grandpa shrugged. "I don't know what to think. That dog is darn annoying as well as a health and safety hazard. At the same time, he's more human than dog. I don't like the idea of him being a prisoner or forced to be on his own."

"Then give him another chance," I pleaded. "He's brainy, and he needs something to do with his brains."

Grandpa took an extra deep breath. He was silent for a while. "Very well," said Grandpa at last. "I've got to give it you, you're a determined lad if ever there was one!"

I gave Grandpa the biggest hug ever.

Once again, Ugly and I have spent a couple of afternoons dropping off the flyers all over our neighborhood. We've been careful not to give them to anyone who hates junk mail. And success! I've had three emails from interested dog owners. I wrote back telling people to bring their dogs at ten o'clock in the morning tomorrow, Saturday, to the park around the corner from Mrs. Manchester's house.

Tonight, being Friday night, I've suddenly become scared stiff about Ugly and me running a dog class. I need to have some good ideas for the first lesson, especially if each dog owner is going to pay me $10. Three people giving me $10 a lesson comes to $30. That's a fortune! I've put a piece of paper and pen next to my bed so that whenever I have a brain wave during the night, I can write it down.

Of course, I've never forgotten the lessons that Maggie Buchan taught Ugly and me back in the first part of this year. They were lessons I have to remember forever. Maggie was the dog expert who Grandpa called in to teach me how to train Ugly when he was out of control. I've been thinking about those first few lessons. I was unbelievably nervous. If Ugly and I did not succeed with the lessons, my parents were going to make me give Ugly away.

The first thing I learned from Maggie was really tough: it was me who needed the training. I had to care for Ugly so he would want to obey me. I had to be the one to feed him, groom him, and exercise him. I have to admit that I'd let Mom do a lot of the boring stuff. But that was the whole point. Ugly loved Mom and not me because she was looking after him so well.

Remembering all this tonight has given me my first training idea. I will get my three dog owners to sit down and answer some important questions. I've written a questionnaire that will show if the dog owners are doing enough to care for their dogs. Here are the questions:

DOG OWNER—
PLEASE TELL THE TRUTH

WHO FEEDS YOUR DOG?

WHO CLEANS UP YOUR DOG'S
POO AND PEE?

HOW OFTEN DO YOU COMB
AND BRUSH YOUR DOG?

HOW OFTEN DO YOU TAKE
YOUR DOG FOR A WALK?

HOW LONG ARE MOST WALKS?
DO YOU LET YOUR DOG TALK
TO OTHER DOGS?
DO YOU TALK TO YOUR DOG?
DO YOU PLAY WITH YOUR DOG?
HAVE YOU TRIED TO TEACH
YOUR DOG GOOD MANNERS?
HOW OFTEN IS YOUR DOG ON
HIS/HER OWN?
WHAT IS YOUR MAIN PROBLEM
WITH YOUR DOG?

I've just read through my questions again. It's a good start. But it might take only five minutes to answer the questions. I think I will give the owners a stern little talk about looking after a dog so he or she will love and obey them—just like Maggie Buchan gave me a bit of a talking-to.

What next? We will need to start the dog obedience

lessons. The list of Maggie's dog training hints! They are right here to remind me, pinned to the wall next to my bed. I wrote them out earlier this year.

- Always be gentle.
- Try not to yell.
- Give rewards, not punishments.
- Have plenty of healthy dog treats in your pocket.
- Reward your dog right away when he obeys you.
- Keep lessons short.
- Break up lessons with some fun and games.
- Repeat the lessons a few times a day and every day.
- Keep commands simple.
- Don't yell at your dog.
- Give lots of praise and pats.

12

I had a bumpy off-and-on sleep last night. In the end, I got up around midnight and read through my clients' emails again. There was Courtney Lee, who had a male nine-month-old Kelpie cross; Baz Murphy, who had a female Maltese cross terrier; and Pippa Wilson, who had a male Labrador.

I already knew what the three dogs looked like: Kelpies are often dark caramel-colored or black and white, and they are supposed to be good sheepdogs. My friend Hugh has a big, roly-poly golden Labrador living next door to him that likes to pull the laundry off its family's clothesline. I googled Maltese terrier—it looked cute and fluffy-white.

But knowing what the dogs looked like wasn't much of a start. These dogs needed training. What were the dogs really like? What were their owners like? Why were the owners desperate enough to write back to a kid's advertisement? Wait a minute. It hit me. My clients didn't know I was a kid.

When I woke this morning, the sky was mostly dark. There was just a thin line of yellow on the horizon. Even the birds were still asleep. My first thought was to choose my clothes and get dressed. I had to look professional. Milly calls it "power dressing." For a start, you wear black or dark blue. Dark colors make other people know you are in charge. I decided on black jeans and a black T-shirt. My sneakers had once been white, but now they were old and a dirty-gray color; I had given them a thick coat of Grandpa's black boot polish.

After this, I started on my hair. I've always had messy hair. It doesn't take to styling. To control it, I used so much of Gretchen's styling gel that my head felt cold, but I got a result. Most of my hair was flat as a pancake, but the front of my bangs was all spiked up like fingers. By the time I'd got "the look" right, the sun had risen.

I was taking one last admiring glance in the bathroom mirror when I noticed Ugly sitting next to me, looking up. (Ugly plods after me absolutely everywhere. If he could squeeze into the toilet with me, he'd do that.) Anyway, Ugly's own hairdo was very unprofessional. It was as messy as mine usually is. If Ugly was going to make a good impression, he needed a "makeover" too.

Ugly's hair was a challenge, but I enjoyed my job as a hair stylist. I plastered it with the last of Gretchen's gel. I gave Ugly a look-alike style—flat on top with a cool, spiky front. I took Mom's hand mirror, crouched next to Ugly, and gazed at the two of us side by side. With our sandy-colored hair and stand-up bangs, we could have been twins. "You look awesome," I said to Ugly. He woofed at his own reflection, then he said "thank you" by giving my face a lick.

Just at that moment, Gretchen walked into the bathroom. At first she was all sleepy and vague. Then she noticed my hair. "That hair makes you look like a cockatoo," she said.

I could feel my spiky hair wilting under her nasty words. But I wasn't going to let my big sister ruin my day. I was thinking up a smart reply when Gretchen took a second glance at Ugly. I reckon he felt like a cool dude with his new hairstyle. He wagged his tail and barked at Gretchen.

"Am I seeing what I think I'm seeing?" asked Gretchen, looking at me and then Ugly.

"Yep," I said proudly.

"Matching hairstyles for a boy and a dog?"

"Yep," I said again.

"Weird," said Gretchen.

Unfortunately, Gretchen next spied the empty hair gel container. "What?" she yelled, her eyes blazing like killer laser beams. I knew it was time for Ugly and me to exit the bathroom. "You selfish little creep!"

After shutting the bathroom door behind us, Ugly and I escaped into the hallway. I walked away, shaking my head in disappointment. When is Gretchen going to grow up?

13

Although Dad was still in a grump about Ugly eating his USB stick, Grandpa was doing his best to forgive Ugly for the rhubarb wrecking. I was grateful he'd agreed to walk to the park with me. "I will be keeping an eye on things," he said that morning. "Anything to keep that mutt out of trouble."

To be ready for his big day, in addition to his morning biscuits, I gave Ugly a duck-egg smoothie. I think this is the sort of energy food Olympic athletes have. Mom made Grandpa and me a cooked breakfast—sausages, eggs, and such. "You both need your strength," she said.

Grandpa, Ugly, and I were waiting at the park

by a quarter to ten. I asked Grandpa to sit on the bench. Ugly and I stood over on the other side of the playground. There were tons of worries and what-ifs making my heart pump away nervously. I was looking in my backpack to check that my questionnaire sheets, pens, and dog treats were all in order, when I felt Ugly tugging at the leash that was looped over my wrist. I glanced up to see a lady about Mom's age with a golden Labrador walk over to Grandpa.

I was certain this was Pippa Wilson. She looked fit and cheerful. She was dressed in bright, colorful clothes. Grandpa pointed my way. I waved. Ugly gave a happy yap. The lady (Ugly's and my very first client) strolled over to me.

"Hi there! This is Sam, and I'm Pippa," she said.

Ugly and Sam sniffed each other in a friendly way. This was a great start.

"I'm Eric, and this here is Ugly," I said. "Ugly will teach your dog, Sam."

Then Pippa smiled a bit sadly and said, "I'm so very sorry. I came to tell you that I've double booked. I have an important painting class today. But I like to see a youngster show a flair for business. Keep at it, young man. Here's five dollars for the late cancellation. We might give you a try further down the road. Let's go, Sam."

I watched Pippa jog along with Sam out of the park. Ugly gave another little yap as if to call to Sam the Labrador, "Hey! Come back!"

With my head and shoulders down, I walked miserably across to Grandpa.

"I'm down to only two customers," I said. "My business will be a disaster—like a party where hardly anyone shows."

Grandpa looked up into the air as if he was thinking—which he was. "If you act cheerfully and like you're sure of yourself, then your two remaining customers will still enjoy themselves. I suggest as soon as the next one turns up, you march up to them, shake hands, and confidently introduce yourself. Let's practice."

There and then, Grandpa gave me a handshaking lesson. Not weak and feeble "like a wet fish" (as Grandpa put it), not bone-crushing "as if you're a caveman," but "firm and friendly." And I had to look people in the eyes and smile while I introduced myself. We must have shaken hands twenty times before Grandpa said I had the hang of it.

At the very moment my handshaking lessons had finished, a monster of a motorcycle roared up to stop next to the park. A tall, broad-shouldered man stepped off it. He swept his helmet from his head and peeled off his enormous gloves. He was as bald as an egg, but he had bushy, black eyebrows and a curling mustache. He wore a leather jacket and jeans as well as thick boots. With his hands pushed into his jacket pockets, he marched over to Grandpa and me.

"Mornin', men. Do you know where this dog training thing is?"

Grandpa gave me a look which clearly said, "You handle this, Eric."

I decided to try out Grandpa's lessons. I stuck my hand out, looked straight into the man's dark-brown eyes, tried my hardest to smile, and said, "Eric Bright is the name. I'm in charge here. How can I help you?"

The biker looked too surprised not to shake my hand. "Baz Murphy," he said. But mid-shake, he threw back his head and bellowed with laughter. My heart sank. "Are you for real?" he asked.

I looked at Grandpa for help, but he shrugged and tilted his head toward the biker as if to say to me, "Go on. You're in charge."

"I'm for real," I said. "What can I do for you?"

"Well, this," said Baz Murphy when he'd stopped laughing. He started to unzip his jacket. What on earth was going on? How to deal with weirdos wasn't one of Grandpa's lessons. Just at that moment, I saw two white, hairy ears, two little, bright-brown eyes, and a tiny, wet, black nose poking out from the biker's jacket. "This here is Sheila. I love her to bits. She might be small, but she's a handful."

"Ah!" I said in my most confident voice. "So this is your Maltese cross. I always say there's no problem with a dog that can't improve even a little." I invited Baz to take a seat next to Grandpa and handed him a pen and question-naire which he finished as fast as Ugly gulps down his dinner.

"There you are," said Baz, handing me his filled-out questionnaire. "See if you can help me."

I looked at Baz's answers. It was easy to see Sheila was well cared for, but there were a couple of not-so-good answers. Sheila didn't go on many walks and didn't get to talk to other dogs. And Baz's main problem with Sheila was she made the neighbors complain because she yapped all the time when Baz was at work.

"Can you sort out my Sheila?" asked Baz.

One of my worries had been there would be some doggish problem I wouldn't have a clue about. But Sheila's yapping was easy to understand. "Your dog is lonely, Baz," I said. "Simple as that."

Baz's eyes went big and round. "You're one smart kid," he said. "But a man's got to work. How can it be any other way for Sheila? I can't take her to work."

"Get her a dog friend," I said. "And take them both for more walks where they can talk to other dogs."

Baz was looking at me as if I was some sort of genius. "Wow, that advice was worth more than ten bucks. Here's twenty," he said, fishing the bills from a pocket inside his jacket. "Thanks a bunch."

I tried not to look stunned, but that's tough when you're holding a fortune in your hands. "No worries," I said. "Next step, put Sheila's leash on, and we can introduce her to Ugly."

Ugly was trying hard to be well-behaved. Grandpa was holding his leash. He was sitting very straight. His tail was thumping the ground in excitement, and he was grinning at Sheila. Ugly looked a bit hurt when Sheila snapped at him, but he gently woofed as if to say, "Let's be friends."

Sheila and Ugly started sniffing each other. Ugly seemed to like Sheila's smell a lot. After a while, she got sick of him sticking his nose at her bits and pieces, so she snapped at him again. But Ugly was very patient. He even rolled on his back, his legs sticking up in the air, so Sheila could have a easier time at smelling him all over.

While the doggy "getting to know you" was going on, our other human customer turned up. I knew who she must be. She was leaning backward, hanging onto the leash with both hands as her Kelpie dragged her along.

14

Courtney Lee was dressed all in white: jeans and matching top. She also wore high-heeled shoes. Despite digging her heels into the grass like tent pegs, she was being hauled along by her dog. Courtney looked like she was about my sister's age, but she was dainty and only about my height. You could tell by her screwed-up face that she was not enjoying "walking" her dog. I know all about dogs who are the boss of their masters—or mistresses. Ugly used to be one of them.

I walked up to Courtney, my hand stretched out, ready to shake. Her dog got to me first. He jumped up on me again and again.

"Get down, you silly dog. Stop that. Please don't. I'm

fed up. Get down. I can't bear this. Stop it now. Don't lick the boy's face, you naughty dog. Simon, stop it! You're a darn nuisance. I've had enough. I can't stand this. If you behaved, I'd take you for more walks," shouted Courtney.

Courtney Lee was breaking lots of rules about dog training. For one, you shouldn't shout at a dog. That's the same as human barking. Secondly, how could Simon understand that long string of sentences? Dogs can only understand single words and short sentences. Although Courtney was pulling on Simon's leash, he sprang at me again. I stepped close and said, "Down!" As I did this, I held my hand up to Simon's face. He fell back, his head tilted to one side and one ear cocked straight up as if to say, "What the heck happened?"

I slipped Simon a dog treat and patted his head, "Good boy, Simon!"

"You've obviously learned how to handle dogs with this expert helping you," said Courtney. "Is that old man over there the trainer?"

"No. Ugly and I are," I said, putting out my hand again. "Eric Bright. At your service." I've been waiting to use those words from *The Hobbit* ever since Mom read the story to me last year. Bilbo Baggins says "At your service" to Gandalf and the dwarves when they visit Bag End, his hobbit hole. "At your service" sounds businesslike.

"How quaint," said Courtney. "All right, if you want to be at my service, then please just tell me where the real Eric is. And who on earth is Ugly?"

"No joking. I'm Eric," I said, smiling my biggest, most confident smile. "And that huge dog over there is my dog, Ugly. This is our training school."

Courtney stared at me, her face was like one big question mark. "That creature looks like a horse. Is it dangerous?"

"He's definitely a dog. And he's as kind as you can get," I said.

Before Courtney could back out, I added, "Come over and meet another satisfied customer."

I started walking back to Grandpa, Baz, Ugly, and Sheila, hoping like anything that Courtney would follow. She did. Simon was so pleased to meet other doggy friends that he bounced and jumped and yapped and sprang and bounced some more—all over Sheila and Ugly who also got very yappy and bouncy. Leashes tangled up, people were calling to their dogs, and in the middle of the hullabaloo, Courtney yelled to Baz,

DOGGY TRANSLATIONS:
HI, HEY, NICE TO MEET YOU,
CAN I SNIFF YOUR BUTT, ETC.

"Are you really going along with this kid's training?"

"Give the boy a fair chance," Baz called back. "He's already solved one of my problems with my Sheila."

Once dogs

103

and leashes were separated, Grandpa and Baz gave Courtney their park bench. I handed her the survey. Grandpa took hold of Simon's leash, then the rest of us moved away to give Courtney time to answer the questions. A few minutes later when I looked over her finished questionnaire, I realized Simon might be even more of a handful than Ugly had ever been.

Apparently Simon chewed anything in sight. He'd destroyed furniture, children's toys, and precious family ornaments. He'd been to the vet twelve times in eighteen months for eating dangerous foods and other non-food items. The vet said that Simon had "dietary indiscretions," which Courtney explained meant that Simon will swallow absolutely anything. And to top it all off, Simon's habit of jumping at people had caused Courtney's auntie to fall down and break her ankle.

"Well?" said Courtney, her arms folded across her chest.

"Firstly, your dog is bored stiff—that's why he chews stuff," I said. "Your dog was born to work, like Ugly here. Simon is an intelligent dog who needs a chance to use his brains. Secondly, you need to be the dog's boss because at the moment Simon doesn't respect you one bit. And thirdly"—I pointed at Courtney's high-heeled shoes—"you need to wear flat shoes when you take Simon for walks so you can run with him and not fall over and break your ankle like your auntie did. You have a dog with lots of brains and energy—and he needs exercise."

"And I'm supposed to pay you for insulting me?" asked Courtney.

How to deal with an angry customer wasn't one of the lessons I'd learned yet. Luckily, I heard Baz's voice boom over my shoulder.

"We all have to suck it up sometimes, lady. The kid makes sense."

Courtney chose to stay, but she said, "Well then, what next?"

What next? This was the tricky bit.

15

It's nine o'clock on Saturday night. I find it hard to believe what really did happen next. It's all so embarrassing. I'm groaning aloud as I write.

Now that I've had a few hours to think back on the day, I know I should have stopped while I was ahead. The trouble was, I knew I hadn't given Ugly the chance to run the dog obedience class. After all, this was supposed to be his business.

"The next stage," I said, "is that my business partner, Ugly, will teach your dogs the most important three lessons—how to sit, stay, and come."

"Your business partner?" asked Courtney, snorting with laughter. "Does that massive pile of fleas talk?"

"Well, actually, Ugly does talk," I said in my politest voice. (Inside I was thinking, "How dare you call my dog nasty names!") I took a deep breath and said, "But Ugly will only talk in dog language today, and he will lead by example. That's how he will teach your dog to behave."

"Okay, lead on, Ugly and Eric!" said Baz in a big, cheerful voice.

"All right then," I said. "Would everyone please line up with their dogs?"

There we were—big Baz standing next to his fluffy little Sheila, trendy Courtney standing next to her bouncy Simon, then me and my ginormous Ugly.

"Rule number one!" I called. "Tell your dog to sit while you gently pull up with the leash and push down on your dog's bottom." I looked along the line of sitting dogs and their owners. The lesson was going awesome.

"Hand your dog one of those treats I gave you, then give it a pat and say, 'Good dog.'"

Baz and Courtney followed my instructions. I patted Ugly who was smiling and behaving very well, and then I slipped him a treat.

"Next step!" I said. "Tell your dog to 'stay.' Put the leash down and slowly walk five feet away."

The three of us dog owners lined up facing our dogs. We looked like two rows of soldiers. I was so proud of Ugly. He sat there, very straight-backed, staring at me with excited eyes, his long tongue hanging sideways out of his mouth. The other dogs copied Ugly and sat there too.

"We will now tell our dogs to come. Watch Ugly," I said.

"Come!" I called in a firm voice.

Ugly leaped toward me like a pea from a peashooter. Then the unplanned part happened. The other two dogs rushed forward too. Ugly twisted sideways to check out what was happening. Little Sheila ran, yipping and yapping, under Ugly's legs. Simon pounced on top of Ugly. The three dogs fell over in a happy, heaving heap. Then up they got, Ugly leading the way, racing through the park toward the street where cars were driving up and down.

"Come!" I called.

"Come, Ugly!" I yelled.

"Ugly! Come now!" I screamed.

No response.

Things were getting dangerous. Any moment the dogs might run onto the road and in front of a car—or just disappear forever. Courtney started running across the grassy park in the direction of the three dogs. Just as I had feared, the heel of her shoe stuck in the dirt.

She fell flat onto her face. Baz sprinted up to Courtney to check on her. Grandpa was now on his feet, limping toward the dogs as fast as his metal hip would let him.

Not only were there three dogs in danger, there were also three humans in my care. I had to fix the situation fast. I had only one trick up my sleeve, but I'm sure my dog trainer, Maggie Buchan, would never, ever have used it. What would she think of me if I did this? She would say Ugly and I had failed the most basic standard of dog obedience. But as Grandpa said later, "Desperate times call for desperate measures."

There was nothing else to do. All I could see of Ugly was his tail disappearing around the corner. I took an enormous breath and then bellowed, "Dinner!"

Ugly reacted in a twinkling. As quickly as it takes to flicker your eyelids, he spun around and tore back toward me. His two new dog friends bolted after him. Yes, Ugly came back, but only because he thought he was going to get a big feed. His career as a dog trainer was over.

16

You might be wondering what happened a few minutes after Ugly returned to me—things like, was Courtney okay? Well, she sort of was and sort of wasn't. Apart from being covered in grass and leaves, there was a smudge of dirt on the end of Courtney's pretty nose where her face had hit the ground. It made her look like she had a dog nose. I thought it best not to tell her that. She also had a sprained ankle. Turns out Baz was a paramedic. He checked Courtney's ankle and said it was okay to walk on.

Grandpa invited Courtney and Baz to come and share a cup of tea at our place. Surprisingly, they both accepted. We locked up the chickens and ducks, and then put Ugly, Sheila, and Simon out in the back to have some fun. They played tag the whole time we were inside.

Even though it was the weekend, Dad had gone to work at the office. He was doing overtime, trying to catch up on the work that disappeared with the USB stick. Mom was out visiting friends, and Gretchen had gone to the city for the day. Grandpa and I had the place to ourselves. He had cooked a batch of fruit scones early that morning. Grandpa, the two clients, and I sat around the kitchen table and had a good old time. Sort of. Grandpa chatted away to Baz and Courtney. I was feeling like such a fool that I didn't say much more than, "Would you like another scone?"

At long last, our guests said it was time to go home with their dogs. Grandpa gave Baz and Courtney each a carton of mixed duck and chicken eggs. I offered Baz his money back, but he told me to keep it. He said he'd enjoyed himself and that he and little Sheila would practice the "sit, stay, come" at home by themselves. "I often find having friends around is a distraction when I'm trying to get an important job done," said Baz. "It's obviously the same with dogs."

Courtney wasn't quite as kind. As Simon was doing his usual thing, pulling on the leash and dragging his owner away, Courtney called over her shoulder, "If you think my dog doesn't respect me, then you need to take a better look at your own dog."

Those words cut deep. At the same time, I had to face the fact that the Ugly and Eric dog training business had injured one of its customers and damaged her clothes. I felt bad about the grass stains on Courtney's white jeans and top. To be honest, a stranger might have thought Courtney had rolled in horse poo. I ran after her, waving my twenty dollars in the air. "Take this for dry-cleaning your clothes!" I called.

Courtney stopped. She looked surprised. "All right then," she said. "Thanks."

It hurt to see my fortune disappear into Courtney's purse, but I knew I'd done the right thing.

●●●

I must have seemed a bit down, because Gretchen was strangely nice to me tonight. She didn't tease me about the failed dog business. She was polite to Ugly. She even played a card game with me before dinner—although that wasn't her idea (I overheard Mom suggest this to her when they were alone in the kitchen). That didn't help much.

TWITCHY EYE

THIS ONLY HAPPENS WHEN DAD IS SUPER CRANKY!

Dad was extra tired and cranky from having worked six long days at the office. "I would have been at home today if it wasn't for that dog," he said, staring angrily at Ugly who was lying behind the sofa. Poor Ugly could tell he was still in trouble with Dad. He looked at Dad with sad eyes, his big ears flat and low, and gave a small whine.

That poor dog knows he's in trouble with me as well. Even though he had an exciting time playing with his dog friends this afternoon, once they left, he kept following me everywhere around the house with his tail between his legs. Five minutes ago, Ugly tried to squeeze himself under the desk in my bedroom so he could be close to me. He's so huge, he almost tipped the desk over, so I've commanded him to lie away from me. He looks sad. I'm not so mad at him—just disappointed. But that isn't fair of me either. How can I expect a dog to understand what Dad calls "business principles"?

ARROOO

"I'M SORRY"
(IN UGLY LANGUAGE)

17

I need to remind myself that the down feeling you get after you lose at something doesn't last forever. Last night, I couldn't see that anything good could happen for Ugly and me—but take today, for example.

Every so often on a Sunday, Grandpa walks to the local graveyard and puts flowers on Grandma's grave. Usually he goes by himself, but this morning he invited Ugly and me to walk with him. "If we walk off a bit of the mutt's energy, he might leave my veggie garden alone."

Our walking route took us past the park. That brought back the memories of yesterday's dog training disaster. I went all quiet. Ugly tried to cheer me up by bouncing about and licking my hand. I absentmindedly patted him on his hairy head.

"You tried really hard yesterday," said Grandpa. "It might seem like you lost, but you behaved like a gentleman by giving your profits to Courtney. Better to be poor but honest than rich and a rascal."

It was comforting to hear this, but something important was getting me down. "What about Ugly?" I asked. "He failed. And Dad is still upset about the USB stick. I feel like he's waiting for a reason to lock Ugly away."

"I don't know what's to be done, lad. You're right about Ugly. Things aren't looking too good for him. And I'm getting a bit tired too," Grandpa said, shaking his head sadly. "If your grandma was still with us, she'd come up with some brilliant idea for the mutt."

I wish I remembered more about Grandma. She had soft skin and smelled like old-lady perfume—violets, I think. She cooked delicious vegetable soup and grew beautiful roses. She played the piano and was just about to start teaching me to play too—but she died. I like to hear Grandpa talk about her.

"Did Grandma know lots about dogs?" I asked.

"My Alyson Marjorie had a heart for all living creatures," said Grandpa. "She loved people and animals. She had a special gift with animals that had suffered at the hands of other humans. They trusted her. She didn't expect anything of them. Animals could just be themselves."

As we walked, we passed the community tennis court and the convenience store, then we turned a corner and headed down a quiet road. About half a mile away, I could see the tall iron gates of the grave-yard. All this time, I was thinking about what Grandpa had just told me about Grandpa.

When we entered the graveyard gates, Grandpa turned right. He wove his way in and out of graves, under the shade of old trees and past bushes where tiny birds played hide-and-seek. Grandpa seemed to forget me. His mind was set on getting to his Alyson Marjorie. And then we were there. Her grave was a little by itself with a small headstone. Under her name were carved the words, GOD IS LOVE.

At the foot of the headstone was a vase with some droopy flowers in it. Grandpa took a bunch of red roses and white daisies wrapped in newspaper out of his tote bag. He knelt down (artificial hip and all), removed the old flowers, filled the vase with water from a jar that he also had in his bag, then arranged the fresh flowers.

"There now, my sweetheart," said Grandpa in a gentle voice. "The first of my early summer roses for you."

It was a soft afternoon. "Soft" is the best word I can think of. It was sunny, but there was a cool breeze—and even the breeze just trickled and didn't blow. Although there were other people visiting graves, they weren't near us. Everyone was quiet. They weeded or just sat on the ground chatting.

Me, Grandpa, and Ugly sat next to Grandma's

grave for quite a while—daydreaming and doing some remembering about Grandma. Ugly rolled on his side and dozed, a bit of his tongue sticking out of his mouth. That's when I discovered something about being really, really quiet; it's when ideas float in from nowhere.

One moment I was thinking about what Grandpa said was Grandma's way of treating animals—*they could just be themselves*—and then it came to me in a flash. My plans for Ugly's career have been what humans might like. Why would Ugly care about whether someone is fit or unfit? He doesn't think about those sorts of things. He only cares about whether someone is kind or not. If my plans for his personal trainer

QUIET TIME WITH GRANDPA AND GRANDMA

business had worked, poor Ugly would not have understood why he had to run and run with a bunch of strangers.

And what about the dog training business? That is what humans want too. You don't see dogs marching around training each other. Ugly just wants to be friends with other dogs, talk dog, and have some fun. I could have trained him more strictly so he was too scared to run off with his friends, but who wants to be forced into a career?

I now had a strong clue about the sort of job that would be best for Ugly. He needed a job he would really love doing; something that comes naturally to a dog.

Believe it or not, a job opportunity came this afternoon when Grandpa, Ugly, and I were strolling back home from our visit to Grandma's grave.

●●●

Part of our route home was past our local convenience store again. It is a little shop nestled between other homes, no other shops around. It has a green door with a bell dangling over the top that rattles and rings when you walk inside. You can hardly see through the front window because it is plastered with flyers advertising services like: "Reliable Babysitter," "Gutters and Lawn Maintenance," "Tennis Club News," "Home Hairdressing," and "Volunteers needed for Church Op Shop." Grandpa stopped to read the advertisements, when a photo of a dog in the bottom corner of the window caught my eye.

It was of a shiny-coated, long-haired, black-and-white collie sitting, back straight, staring with big, loving eyes at the camera. Above the photo was the word "Missing," and below was written:

REWARD

BELOVED FAMILY PET, CHARLIE.

SEVEN YEARS OLD.

CONTACT THE MCCAW FAMILY AT:

ALLTHEMCCAWS@SOLONG.COM

18

This advertisement for the missing Charlie McCaw is a solution to Ugly's problems. The McCaws live about ten doors down our street, on the other side. Little Alex McCaw is in third grade at school. At dinner tonight, I told my family about the "Missing" poster. Then I announced that Ugly is going to have a new career—lost dog finder. Amazingly, this was Ben Segala's idea for a dog job. It's right there on the school survey.

"Think of all the dogs that go missing," I said. "Ugly gets along well with dogs. I think he'd be good at sniffing and tracking. This job was made for him."

Mom made polite, not very interested noises like, "Ohhh…ahh…mmm."

Gretchen rolled her eyes with a "not again" look.

"How about Ugly becomes a lost USB stick finder?" said Dad in a grumpy voice.

"I think we've given this career thing enough of a try for the moment. Give us a break, Ec," said Grandpa.

"But Grandpa," I said, "it was you who told me, 'Never say die.' And Miss Jolly said to never, ever, ever, ever, ever give up! I think I got the number of 'evers' wrong. But I bet Sir Winston Churchill would tell Ugly and me to be the best lost-dog finders ever!"

"Seems sensible to

give up when you've had as many failures as you've had, Eccle," said Gretchen in a bored, flat sort of voice. "Even Winston Churchill might regard you as the exception to the rule."

"Easy does it, Gretchen," said Mom in a warning way. She turned to me. "Ec, a 'break' does not mean giving up."

"But this all started because Dad said he'd either tie up Ugly in the backyard or lock him in an enclosure," I said. "I can't let that happen. Ugly has to have a job that keeps him out of trouble."

"That dog is still causing arguments," said Dad. "Now you're expecting Grandpa to give his free time to every one of your ridiculous ideas. It would make life easier for everyone if Ugly was outside and restrained for a part of each day and evening. He'd get used to it, Ec."

"Your dad isn't a cruel man, Eccle," said Mom. "But take a look at the size of Ugly. He's the biggest dog I've ever known! We really need a bit of peace and a lot more space in this house."

"Restrained." What a scary word. It reminds me of a convict in chains.

I had to control myself if I was going to save Ugly from such a terrible fate. I told myself to speak slowly and calmly. I took a deep breath and said, "Everyone is worried about Grandpa. I get that. This next job, Ugly and I can mostly do on our own."

"How's that?" asked Dad.

"Because Grandpa won't have to waste his time keeping an eye on me. You all know the McCaws. And Mrs. Manchester next door is really good friends with Nanna McCaw, who lives in a little apartment behind their place. They share cake recipes and get together to crochet stuff like tea cozies. So there's no stranger danger."

"Yes, yes," said Mom. "The McCaws are a good family, but what's your plan?"

I had thought this through, thank goodness. I explained that I'd visit the McCaw family and ask them to let Ugly sniff their dog's belongings. Then I'd take Ugly for a walk to see if he could track Charlie.

Mom and Dad laid down some rules.

"Grandpa has to go with you to the McCaws' to properly discuss your idea," said Mom.

"As for the tracking walk, you're only allowed to do it in daylight," said Dad.

"And take two school friends," said Mom.

"And stick within a half mile of home," said Dad.

"And no talking to strangers," said Mom.

I said "yes" to everything.

19

This morning, right after Monday assembly at school, I asked Milly and Hugh to meet me at recess for an ordinary general meeting. We've had so many meetings. I couldn't call this one extraordinary anymore.

We met on the seat under our favorite pepper tree. I had only just begun telling my friends about needing their help with Ugly's sniffer job when Barnaby turned up. He was waving his hands and jumping about in an overexcited way. I should have been more patient with him, but I badly needed to discuss Ugly.

"We are having an important meeting, Barnaby.

If you want someone to play with, then go look somewhere else," I said in a strict voice.

"Hey, Barnaby, what about finding Alderney?" suggested Hugh in a much friendlier way. "She's being a giraffe again. You could be a sloth."

Barnaby would not budge. He started making upset noises and searching about in the pockets of his shorts and sweater.

"Barnaby, this is private. You can play with me at lunchtime," said Milly.

Barnaby called out, "Ugwee!"

"Yes, we are having a meeting about Ugly," I said. "Now please leave us alone!"

"Ugwee!" said Barnaby, pulling something out of his pocket. He shoved it at me. When I looked, I saw the piece of the torn picture of Ugly. It looked like it had been ironed to smooth out the scrunched-up creases. Hugh and Milly leaned across to look.

There was half of Ugly's head, one eye, and two

ears pricked up like he does when he's concentrat-ing. You could also see his DOG HERO medal shining on his big, brave, hairy chest.

BARNABY'S FAVORITE PHOTO OF "UGWEE"

Barnaby grinned. He pointed at the picture and shoved it toward me. "Ugwee!"

Out of the corner of my eye, I saw Miss Jolly stand-ing nearby. She was smiling and nodding at Barnaby. She must have helped Barnaby come up with a way to fix things up between us. Barnaby was giving me back the torn picture that he'd tried to mend.

But what did I do? That picture of Ugly getting his bravery medal from the Manchester family was precious. You can't repeat a special day like that. Instead of feeling grateful, I felt angry all over again. A couple of weeks ago, I threw out the part of the picture that I had ended up with after Barnaby had tugged it apart. I wanted the whole picture again—all perfect—not this piece. I started to turn away. "Yeah, you can keep it," I said. "It's not the real picture."

"Eccle!" said Milly in a shocked voice. "The smoothed-out piece of the picture is Barnaby's way of saying 'sorry.'"

"You're not being fair, Ec," said Hugh.

"I never thought you'd hang onto a grudge this long," said Milly.

"I bet this is how wars start and then go on and on," said Hugh.

My friends don't often tell me off. I knew what they said was right. If I couldn't get over a picture being wrecked, how could I expect people to forgive each other for truly enormous things? How silly and mean I must have seemed to my friends. I took hold of the picture and said as politely as I could, "Thanks, Barnaby."

I knew my quick "thank you" wasn't as good as it

could be. Deep down inside me, a little voice was telling me off. It wasn't just Barnaby who'd ripped my photo. I had also been part of my picture getting ripped. If I'd let Barnaby keep it for a bit longer, my Ugly picture would still be in one piece. I took a deep breath. "I'm also sorry, Barnaby. I hung onto Ugly's picture, so I guess I ripped it too," I admitted.

Milly smiled her gap-toothed smile. Hugh gave me the thumbs-up. Barnaby looked happy. He laughed and skipped off—the sort of slow, careful skip you make when you're just learning.

It didn't take long to finish our meeting. Hugh and Milly liked the idea of helping Ugly and me find Charlie, the lost dog. All they had to do now was get permission from their parents to join us.

20

This afternoon, as soon as I got back from school, Grandpa and I walked down with Ugly to knock on the McCaws' door. Mr. McCaw answered. He is a big man with a smiley face. "Goodness me! What a pleasant surprise! The Bright family and their famous dog, Ugly," said Mr. McCaw. "Come right in—all three of you. I will get Ugly a bowl of water."

Sitting in the McCaw kitchen with young Alex, his parents, and Nanna McCaw, I explained the reason for our visit. When I said I hoped Ugly might track down the McCaws' dog, Alex started to cry. That set off all the McCaws. Even big Mr. McCaw had tears in his eyes. Ugly walked across to sit right next to Alex. He plonked a paw on Alex's knee as if to say, "There, there. I'm so sorry for you."

"I want my brother back," sobbed Alex.

Ugly gave a loud, sympathetic whine.

"You lost your brother too?" I asked.

"Charlie is my brother," said Alex. Then he ran out of the kitchen, Mrs. McCaw following.

"He's an only child," explained Nanna McCaw.

"Not that we wanted it that way," said Mr. McCaw. "That's just how it turned out. Alex and his dog, Charlie, have grown up together."

Grandpa took out his handkerchief, blew his nose, and then stared at his feet. I felt tears prickling my eyes. Ugly gave a little, sad howl. Finding Charlie McCaw was no longer just a way for Ugly to prove he can have a career; it was a very, very serious problem that I badly wanted to fix. I explained to Nanna and Mr. McCaw my plan to have Ugly sniff out Charlie McCaw.

"Ugly and I can't promise to find Charlie," I said, "but we will give it our best try. Ugly is intelligent, nosey, and doesn't give up. That's what gets him into trouble with my family, but it shows that a habit that's annoying can be used for good things too. Please give him a chance."

"Go for it, Eric," said Mr. McCaw, "but I don't want to get our Alex's hopes up. We will tell him the truth—that Ugly has not been professionally trained for this work, but that you and he will try. Can we help in any way?"

I had this all thought out. I explained I needed a picture of Charlie and an object that smelled strongly of him. Mr. McCaw gave me a copy of the "Missing" poster in the convenience store window. He also offered me either a dog blanket, a favorite bone, or a rubber chew toy. I chose the blanket. On our way out, I said to Mr. McCaw, "Please tell Alex that I'm feeling really sad for him."

CHARLIE'S THINGS

TASTY BONE

CARROT CHEW TOY

FAVORITE BLANKET

MISSING

CHARLIE
IF FOUND PLEASE
EMAIL:
MC_CAW@PELMEL.COM

MISSING POSTER

"Very kind of you." Mr. McCaw smiled. He shook Grandpa's and my hands.

When we got home this evening, Ugly and I went straight to the backyard where I began teaching him. This has to be the fastest training session in history. Ugly and I have only a couple of afternoons to achieve what the professionals might do in weeks or months. Whatever has happened to Charlie McCaw, we have to find him sooner than weeks or months—or there is probably no hope.

21

It's been two days since I last wrote in this book. That was the day Grandpa, Ugly, and I got back from our visit to the McCaws' place. Right after I got home, I had to work out ways to teach Ugly to be a professional sniffer dog. My plan was to get expert information later that night about sniffer dog training from Maggie Buchan. She's the dog trainer who taught me how to treat Ugly properly and how to train him. Maggie lives way over on the western coast. Unfortunately, I couldn't even call her. Grandpa told me Maggie has gone camping up in the mountains, way out of cell-phone range. Instead, I've had to get information from the internet.

According to what I have read, to train a sniffer dog, you let the dog smell the object, then you reward him—lots and lots of times. I've been shoving Charlie McCaw's blanket against Ugly's nose, then patting him and giving him a treat—or sometimes playing ball with him for a few seconds. That way, Ugly is supposed to enjoy the smell of Charlie McCaw, because it means food or fun.

Ugly really does find the new game fun. He buries his nose in Charlie's blanket and wags his tail like a windmill. Sometimes, he gives an excited yelp as if to say, "This stinky dog smell is interesting. I'd like to meet the owner of this smell."

Today, about twenty minutes after playing the sniff-and-treat game, I put Ugly in the house then hid the blanket in a huge bush growing against the fence. After this, I led Ugly back outside and told him, "Find the blanket! Where's the blanket?"

Ugly ran straight to the bush, squeezed into the

RUFF!

CHARLIE'S
STINKY
BLANKET

DOGGY TRANSLATION:

THIS STINKY DOG
SMELL IS INTERESTING.
I'D LIKE TO MEET THE
OWNER OF THIS <u>SMELL</u>!

middle and came back with Charlie's blanket. I praised him lots. Even the chickens and ducks got excited. They made a heck of a racket, as if they were cheering Ugly.

Like I said, the training has needed to be as quick as that. I know that finding Charlie's blanket might have been luck, or that another time Ugly might get sick and tired of this new "game." But we can't waste a minute. It is a risk with such speedy training, but we need to begin the hunt for Charlie tomorrow. Tonight, I got on the phone and called Milly and Hugh. So far things are going smoothly; my friends are allowed to help me and Ugly search for Charlie McCaw after school finishes tomorrow.

22

Right after school this afternoon, with a promise that we would be back by dark, the four of us—Milly, Hugh, Ugly, and me—said goodbye to our parents. Milly's dad, Hugh's mom, and my parents stood on the sidewalk outside our place waving to us. Mom had invited Mr. Dunn and Mrs. Cravenforth to stay for some lemonade; I wished they would just go inside. It wasn't as if we were explorers sailing for the other side of the world.

We walked up the sidewalk past Mrs. Manchester's place. She was getting her mail out of the mailbox.

"I've heard all about this rescue mission from

Nanna McCaw," said Mrs. Manchester. "I wish you the very best of luck."

"Thank you, Mrs. Manchester," I said in my most grown-up voice.

I wouldn't turn around to look for our parents, but Milly did.

"Are they going inside?" I asked.

"Not yet," said Milly. "Oh, wait. Yes, they're moving away now."

"Good. Now we can concentrate. Milly, did you remember the spare leash?"

"Yes, of course I have. You made me put it in my backpack. Why are you asking?"

"That's what you do in an important search-and-rescue operation. You have to check and double-check," I explained.

"Well then, do you have Charlie McCaw's blanket?" asked Milly.

"You can see I'm carrying it!" I said.

"Just double-checking," said Milly.

"Hugh, do you still have the dog first aid kit?" I asked.

"Yep," said Hugh. "And some chocolate for us in case we get hungry and tired."

"Good thinking," I said. "And Hugh, please hold up the 'Lost Dog' sign a bit higher."

I had glued the poster of Charlie McCaw onto a piece of cardboard and nailed it to the stick of an old broom. If we carted the sign around, it might jog people's memories without us even having to ask if they'd seen Charlie. I was holding on to Ugly, who was pulling excitedly on a long leash. This time, I was not expecting Ugly to walk at heel. I wanted him to be free to sniff.

Ugly loved the sniffing. He dragged me into bushes, around trees, and he even tried to get me to go into people's properties. I had promised my parents we wouldn't do that. We had to stay on the sidewalks.

Still, it was a good time of day to do our search and

rescue. Big kids were strolling home, slow and tired, from high school; grown-ups who caught the bus home from the train station after a day's work in the city were also walking along. Then, there were the joggers, running before dinnertime, the cyclists, the moms pushing strollers, and the dog walkers. Like birds sing just before sunset, humans seem to get active too.

The sign that Hugh was carrying got us a bit of attention.

"I've seen that collie dog," said a man in a business suit, "but he was with his owners a long time back. Good luck, kids."

"Dog! Dog!" said a little boy sitting up in his stroller. When his mother explained the dog was lost, he said, "Poor dog."

A tall boy from the high school stopped and stared closely at the sign. "That poster is at the convenience store. It's been up for a week. Don't like your chances. No harm in trying, I guess."

The rest of the time, Ugly just about pulled my arm off, especially when it came to meeting other dogs. We went up and down and around streets I'd never been into before. We followed small lanes until they became dead ends. Most of the time, I let Ugly lead the way. My heart kept leaping up when he'd have his nose glued to the ground and drag me along with him as if he was onto something. But the something was never Charlie McCaw—it was usually more like dog poo. Our feet were sore. We were getting tired. Even sharing Hugh's chocolate bar didn't give us much more energy.

Eventually, the summery daylight dimmed. We knew we had to get home quickly. The walking home was more of the same—letting Ugly sniff anywhere he wanted. There was only one moment when he got incredibly excited. We were passing the park that is around the corner from Mrs. Manchester's house.

Ugly started pulling toward the park, furiously sniffing the grass, then he tugged so hard the leash came out of my hand. He galloped toward some trees and a large clump of low bushes growing along Mrs. Manchester's boundary. Had he found Charlie? Was that poor lost dog lying injured, maybe even dying, somewhere under the bushes? Ugly dived and scrambled into the branches and twigs. Milly, Hugh, and I heard Ugly's snuffling and scuffling. Next, we heard growling. Then, a terrible howl came from Ugly.

I raced toward the spot where Ugly had disappeared and began to push my way into the bushes. At that moment, Ugly leaped out. A ginger cat was clinging to his back, clawing and hissing. It was Mrs.

PENELOPE'S REVENGE!

HISSS!

Manchester's Penelope. Ugly ran around in circles, trying to shake Penelope off, but she held on like a rodeo rider. Only when Ugly rolled onto the ground did Penelope jump off and sprint homeward in an angry streak. Ugly limped toward me. The first thing I noticed was the blood on his face. He had a cut just under his eye, and his nose had a drip of blood hanging off it like red snot.

23

I t's hard to believe the sniffer-dog hunt for Charlie McCaw was just this afternoon. We were a sad bunch as we headed back to my place. Once back home, Hugh dumped the "Lost Dog" sign on our front porch. The four of us—Hugh, Milly, Ugly, and me—stepped inside, tired and quiet.

My friends and I were getting ready to tell our families that our search and rescue expedition had failed—that it had been a catastrophe. But we didn't have to. Once we were in the living room, Dad took one look at us and said, "Oh dear!"

Milly's dad said, "No need to ask questions."

Hugh's mom said, "You look like you've just done battle!"

Grandpa said, "Never say die, me hearties!"

Gretchen muttered something I couldn't hear, but Mom said nothing.

She hurried off to the bathroom and brought back the first aid kit.

I thought Mom was going to look after poor Ugly's bleeding nose, but it was me she headed for first. I hadn't realized I'd gotten a big red scrape across my neck when I'd pushed into the bushes to save Ugly.

As for Ugly, he went to the kitchen where he drank about half a bucket of water, then he came back and flopped on the floor behind the sofa. The final proof of how sad and disappointed we all looked was that Gretchen made chocolate mikshakes for Hugh, Milly, and me. If I'd had the energy, I would have taken a picture of the moment.

Gretchen's thoughtfulness didn't help for too long.

Hours of searching the neighborhood, and we had not found a single clue to the whereabouts of Charlie McCaw. By the time we'd finished our drinks and were staring down into our empty glasses, the feelings of failure hit hard all over again.

Grandpa, Mr. Dunn, and Mrs. Cravenforth said comforting things to us. Trouble was, we kids knew they were trying to make us feel better. The talk died down completely—three kids and six grown-ups sitting in silence. All I could think of was little Alex McCaw who would be missing his dog-brother, Charlie.

Then. *Ring-ring.* Mom answered the phone.

"You're kidding! Goodness me! How on earth…? Yes, right away… What? How is he…? What a shame… A miracle… I will. I will. Poor old thing…Wonderful. Wonderful."

It's not polite to listen to other people talk on the phone, but not one of us in the room could pretend we weren't listening. Who on earth was Mom speaking to? What did she mean by a shame and a miracle—all at the same time? Mom finished the phone conversation. Turning to face us all, she said, "Charlie McCaw is home!"

Every person in the room stood and cheered. Ugly came out from his hiding place behind the sofa and started woofing. We fired questions at Mom all at once. I will never forget what Mom said next. "And Ugly and you kids are the reason Charlie is back with his family."

The noise. The clapping. The barking. The jumping about. The hugging. More questions. I can't figure out what came first or last. But the story eventually came out.

It seems many more people than we realized noticed our search-and-rescue mission. An enormous, hairy dog like Ugly, three kids, and a missing dog poster on the end of a broomstick had attracted a lot of attention in our neighborhood. Word quickly spread. Witnesses either told or called other people. Before you could say Jack

Robinson (whoever he is), a lady called Betty Muldoon turned up on the McCaws' doorstep with Charlie.

Betty lives two suburbs away and hadn't seen the reward poster on our convenience store window. Charlie had turned up at her front door—a fractured leg, skinny ribs, and ripped ear, missing his identification tag. It's still anyone's guess how Charlie got into this state, but the kind lady took Charlie to her vet, left a message on the community noticeboard, and has done her best to nurse Charlie back to reasonable health.

Mom had just finished explaining the last part of Charlie's adventures when the doorbell rang. Dad went to answer it. He was back, quickly followed by every single one of the McCaw family—Mr. and Mrs. McCaw, Nanna McCaw (carrying a plate of homemade cookies), Alex, and Charlie McCaw.

Ugly gave Charlie a big welcome. Those two dogs bounced about the living room. Ugly knocked a mug off the coffee table, but he didn't get into trouble. Mom

UGLY + CHARLIE FINALLY SAY HI!

SNIFF SNIFF

SNIFF SNIFF

made a cheese platter. Charlie snuck a bit, but no one yelled at him. Ugly kept plodding up to Alex McCaw, leaning against him, and looking up with a friendly smile. He was saying, "Hey, Alex, I'm happy for you too!"

We invited Mrs. Manchester over to join the celebration. She brought one of her passion fruit sponge cakes. Now we were fourteen people and two dogs. Grandpa made sure there were cups of tea. Dad helped too by serving cold drinks. I opened a box of doggy treats for Ugly and Charlie. We have had such a party tonight. And here I am, writing at almost midnight when I should be in bed asleep. I'm going to be wrecked tomorrow, but who cares? I'm still on a high. I will never, ever forget the moment when our party ended. It was time for everyone to go home. Little Alex McCaw stood at our front door and said to Hugh, Milly, Ugly, and me, "Thank you for helping to find my brother."

24

It's been two weeks since Charlie McCaw came home. A week ago, I took this book to school for Miss Jolly to read. I thought maybe all Ugly's troubles were over—and that this book was now finished. I was wrong. I don't know if my story will have a happy ending.

The day after I'd given this to Miss Jolly, she asked me to stay inside for five minutes at recess. I thought I might be in trouble. It was the opposite.

"Last night, I couldn't put your story down, Eric," said Miss Jolly. "I don't say this lightly, but when it comes to writing, you are gifted. And this book shows a mature development since the one you wrote at the start of the year."

I would like to have said something very grown-up, but I went all shy.

"Thanks, Miss Jolly," I said.

"Is this book finished?"

"I thought it was."

"Why isn't it?"

"We—Ugly and me—were treated like stars until late yesterday. But Dad has started getting cranky with Ugly again. He says Ugly is like a herd of bulls in a china shop. We can't put him out in the back on his own for long. He howls like he's at a funeral till it drives every-one bonkers."

"Well, here's your book back," said Miss Jolly. "Keep on going—with both the writing and finding your dog a job. Don't give up."

"Like the great Sir Winston Churchill said?" I asked.

"Exactly!" said Miss Jolly.

•••

I know Ugly needs to get going on his lost dog rescue job again. The trouble is, even though I've been checking in the local newspaper and at the convenience store for more lost dog notices, there just aren't any. That's a really good thing for dogs and their families, but for Ugly and me, it's what Grandpa calls "a dead-end career."

Sometimes I understand why Dad can get upset with Ugly. When Ugly lies down, even if he tries to choose a spot away from people, parts of him (like a back leg or a front paw) can stick out and trip you up. If Ugly gets excited (and he does that when the family comes home from work or school or if there's a visitor), he knocks things off the coffee table with his wagging tail. He has no use for objects like a cup or an ornament, but he knows humans care about silly things like that. He looks really sorry when he bumps or breaks something.

But Dad just won't let up on Ugly. Poor Ugly has been trying to be good, but he can't do one thing right. I said exactly that to Mom. She explained to me that Dad's boss is putting a lot of pressure on him. Dad is still trying to catch up on the work that disappeared inside Ugly. "Your father really does need the house to be calm and quiet."

After Mom told me about Dad needing everything peaceful, I've been keeping Ugly in my room as much as possible, but it's getting smelly in here. I've been trying to think of something useful for Ugly to do outside. That's why I have to try this next idea. It comes from a problem Grandpa is having with his vegetable garden.

As he's forever telling people, Grandpa is incredibly proud of his garden. For most of the year, he keeps us supplied with crisp, fresh vegetables. Grandpa's problem is that some creature has been digging up the garden and munching the plants. It's definitely not

Ugly. My dog is not a vegetarian. It isn't the chickens and ducks either. We have double-checked. But I finally figured out what the creature was.

Really early this morning when it was more night than day, Ugly poked me awake with his nose. He usually does this because he wants to go outside to go pee. I will be curled up asleep, and Ugly will prod my hand, my back, my neck, or my cheek. If I pretend not to notice, he will jab away even more. He will follow this with plonking his paw down on me.

This time when Ugly woke me, I yawned and groaned, then stumbled out of bed. As I passed through the living room to get to the kitchen's back door, I glanced out the window. A bit of moon shone. The edge of the world had a thin line of light. What I saw down in the backyard explained Grandpa's vegetable-eating invader.

A large gray rabbit was hopping around the garden as if he owned the place. Now and then, he would dig furiously as if he'd discovered gold. Next, the rabbit skipped across to Grandpa's bed of spinach, did some nibbling, and then moved on to munch the broccoli and cauliflower. These particular veggies look like huge white and green flowers. Apart from his precious rhubarb, the broccoli and cauliflower is what Grandpa calls the "jewel in the crown" of his vegetable garden. This rabbit certainly knows how to hurt Grandpa's feelings.

I rushed through the kitchen, Ugly trotting close to me, and opened the back door. "Chase that rabbit!" I whispered to Ugly. I was pointing to the vegetable garden, but Ugly couldn't see what I was showing him. He looked up at me with his little eyebrows pulled together as if he was asking a question. "Off you go, boy!" Ugly ran down the steps. I watched the rabbit freeze.

When Ugly reached the grass, he lifted his back leg against a fruit tree. At the same moment, he must have either smelled or seen the rabbit. Ugly dropped his leg mid-pee and bounded toward the vegetable garden, yapping excitedly. The rabbit rocketed across the lawn toward the back fence. Ugly chased after him. The invader escaped through a hole in the fence. Ugly ran in excited little circles, sniffing the ground like a bloodhound. Grandpa's chickens squawked away and the ducks quacked as if they were saying, "Good job, Ugly!"

At breakfast, Ugly was the hero again. He had saved more of Grandpa's cauliflower and broccoli from

THE
DASTARDLY
VEGETABLE
THIEF!

getting eaten. Grandpa, Mom, and Gretchen patted him and told him he was a star. Even Dad mumbled to Ugly, "Well done, dog."

"There's Ugly's next job," I said. "Rabbit hunter and veggie-patch security guard. It's amazing. Merri Spalding at school suggested this job. I remember her saying that her neighbor's dog guards his family's vegetable garden."

"Good idea," said Dad. "You and Ugly will have to get an early start though. That rabbit obviously times his visits for when we are all fast asleep."

"You'll have to get up at dawn every morning, Ec," said Grandpa.

"It'll do you good getting up extra early," said Mom.

"That means you'll have to go to bed really

THE
VALIANT VEG-PATCH
PROTECTOR!

early like you did when you were three years old, or it will wear you out," said Gretchen with a teasing smile.

"But it's all for a good cause," said Grandpa. "Protecting the family food. That's what it boils down to."

Go to bed early? I'm not a little kid! And get up even earlier than I already do? No way. I already get up early enough to give Ugly a poo walk and his breakfast. I had to do some quick thinking. Sometimes getting up really, really early is okay—but not every morning. Not when it's more night than day. Besides, it's pretty obvious that too many of Ugly's jobs are turning out to be more like my jobs.

"I will give it some thought," I said.

That's an excuse Dad sometimes uses on me when I ask him a favor and he wants to wriggle out of saying "yes." I needed time to talk this over with Milly and Hugh at school. I decided to call an emergency lunch-time meeting.

25

We'll need to have a meeting with Barnaby there," said Milly at recess. "Hugh and I are Barnaby's buddies today."

"I'm not sure he'll want to be part of a meeting," said Hugh, shrugging. "Meetings can be boring."

"I just wish Barnaby would speak, so he could tell us what he's thinking," I said. "He might have some good ideas about Ugly."

It's true. I'd actually like to be real friends with Barnaby, but he's still doing things that make me fed up with him. This morning, we had art. Barnaby was drawing this amazing picture of a city at night with fireworks in the sky. I could tell he didn't have enough colors in his own felt pen set, so I let him borrow my best felt pens. But what did he do to make the fireworks? He jabbed the paper with my pens until some of the tops went all squashy and floppy. When I tried to explain to Barnaby why you should be careful with stuff you borrow, he started flapping his hands about and crying. Then he ran out of the classroom.

Anyway, when I suggested the meeting, I'd forgotten Hugh and Milly were going to play with Barnaby today. Since Milly and Hugh told me I was treating Barnaby unfairly, I've been making an effort to be grown-up. I try hard to be friendly and not say mean things. But I haven't felt like being Barnaby's lunchtime buddy for ages. I wish I could get along with him like Hugh and Milly and some of my other classmates do.

"Could we have a walking meeting?" I asked. "That lets Barnaby move around and play with other kids if he wants to."

"Good idea," said Milly. "I saw a scientist on TV say that walking is good for thinking."

Hugh laughed. "Let's go!"

Maybe the scientists who were experts on walking and thinking did not mean walking around with Barnaby. Sometimes he doesn't just walk, he runs. Of course, we have to run too. But try having a conversation while you run. It's next to impossible. On top of that, Barnaby messed up other kids' games, so we had to sort out the trouble as well as comfort Barnaby who got upset when those kids got angry with him.

By the time I managed to explain to Milly and Hugh about my family expecting me to get up at dawn to help with Ugly's veggie garden job, it was almost the end of lunch. It was hopeless. Milly and Hugh didn't have a chance to come up with helpful ideas. Not only that, as soon as Barnaby heard me talking about Ugly, he got over-the-top excited. He started dragging me by the sleeve toward the coatroom where we hang our bags from pegs.

I let Barnaby pull me along. I was thinking that Barnaby probably feels really lonely. I reminded myself how lonely I used to feel before I got Ugly for my eighth birthday. It must be terrible not being able to talk about your feelings. It would make me cranky. After all, getting my feelings down on paper when I was angry and sad is the main reason I started out as a writer.

Because Milly and Hugh followed us, there were now four people in the coatroom. Barnaby was scrabbling about in his bag.

"What are you looking for, Barnaby?" I asked.

"Ugwee," said Barnaby.

"What do you mean?" asked Hugh.

"You've already given me that piece of Ugly's picture," I said.

Barnaby didn't answer. He pulled out his wallet and opened it. There, inside the clear plastic pocket was the most beautiful drawing of Ugly.

BARNABY IS AN ARTISTIC GENIUS!

"Awesome!" said Hugh. "Look at his hairy head and his smile."

"You know right away it's Ugly," said Milly. "Barnaby's even drawn the medal."

I would love to be able to draw like Barnaby can. "Wow," I said. "How do you do it? Would you show me how you draw dogs sometime?"

Barnaby gave me a quick look straight in the eyes. It's the first time he's ever done that. He smiled and nodded.

"Gee, thanks," I said.

Barnaby kissed the drawing. I realized all over again how lucky I am to have such a wonderful dog as Ugly.

Here was a kid who only has a dog drawing to be friends with. Next thing, Barnaby handed me his drawing.

"For me?" I asked.

Barnaby smiled, clapped his hands, and bounced about on his toes.

"Thanks a million," I said. "Maybe you will have your own dog one day, Barnaby."

Barnaby grinned. I held up my hand and we high-fived. The bell rang for the end of lunch.

As for missing out on Milly and Hugh's advice about how to avoid getting up before the sun, I know I just have to "stand on my own two feet," as Grandpa puts it. I'll figure something out.

The life lessons are coming thick and fast. By taking things a bit more slowly, a solution slipped into my mind as I was sitting up in bed just now writing about today. I'm going to set my alarm clock for early dawn, let Ugly out to guard the veggie garden, and go back to bed. Simple. And clever.

26

I haven't been doing any writing in forever. It's true what I wrote in the last chapter. My plan to get Ugly to guard the veggie garden while I slept *was* simple and clever.

That first early morning, I was half asleep when I let Ugly into the backyard. A duck gave a cranky quack, as if to say, "It's a bit early, Ugly!" I staggered back to bed and slept like a baby until it was time to get ready for school. Ugly was surprisingly happy in the back. I had wondered if he'd get bored and scratch at the kitchen door, but he didn't.

As the days went by, occasionally I'd hear Ugly

yap in my sleep, but none of the family was woken by him being a vegetable garden guard dog. Because Ugly was getting more exercise, he was not as bouncy at night. That made Dad happy. As for Grandpa's veggie garden, I'd been finding it strange that his broccoli and cauliflower were still getting nibbled—perhaps not quite as much as before, but the raiding rabbit had not stopped having a daily snack. Two weeks ago, I discovered the reason.

It was a school day. I'd let Ugly out the back door, but when I went back to bed, I couldn't go to sleep again. Perhaps it was because we were having a times table test that day. I'm not sure. The point is, I got up and decided to walk to the kitchen for a drink. On my way through the living room, I gazed out the big window that looks down on the backyard. What I saw was something my family and even Milly and Hugh wouldn't at first believe when I told them later. I don't blame them. I wouldn't have believed such a story either.

My Dog Gets a Job

I was watching something I've never read or heard about. I'm telling the honest truth. Down there on the lawn was my big, fierce Ugly—the veggie garden guard dog—playing hide-and-seek with the gray rabbit. Ugly would crouch down, and then the rabbit would twitch and skip away behind a bush. Next thing, the rabbit would come flying out, do a big circle, and race up behind Ugly who would pretend to get a fright. He would twist around, crouch again, and the rabbit would spring off behind another bush. On and on this went until I heard Mrs. Manchester's back door slam. The chickens and ducks got scared. They made a hysterical din. In an instant, Ugly's rabbit friend shot across the

WHAT WAS THAT?!

HOP

HE HE HE!

UGLY AND THE RABBIT'S
WEIRD GAME OF
HIDE-AND-SEEK!

NO ONE WILL
EVER BELIEVE
THIS!!!

lawn and under the fence that goes into the reserve that's at the back of our place.

How could I be upset with Ugly? We all need friends. I said that to Grandpa later. He agreed. That weekend, Grandpa got inventive and made wire lids like enormous tea cozies for his most precious vegetables. This way they still get sun and rain, but Ugly's rabbit friend can't get at them.

My family thinks that Ugly having a rabbit friend is a great joke. They've been telling everyone they know. But they've also come home from work with stories other people have told them about amazing friendships between different types of animals. A man at Mom's work once saw a fox and a cat play hide-and-seek just like Ugly did with the rabbit.

All these unusual stories about animals are interesting, but I don't like Ugly being laughed about so much. Ugly is such an amazing dog. He deserves some respect.

27

Some good news and some sad news. Dad's boss has started being nice to Dad again. Because of all the overtime Dad has been doing, he has now caught up with the work lost on the swallowed USB stick. Not only that, the boss says Dad has done a better job than before. The pressure is off Dad, but he says the stress of it all has left him exhausted.

The sad news is that for the last four days, Ugly's rabbit friend has not appeared. I'm worried Mrs. Manchester's cat might have caught it. Mom has tried to comfort me. She says that the rabbit might have been a pet that has now found its way home again. I hope so.

I've tried putting Ugly out the back in the early morning just to let him get some exercise. Trouble is, Ugly doesn't have his rabbit friend to make him race around. He gets bored. He barks at imaginary enemies and then bangs on the back door for me to let him in. That gets Grandpa's fowls all stirred up and noisy. My family is getting woken up by Ugly's silly behavior.

Last night, Ugly was back to being too bouncy for Dad's liking. Dad was looking white-faced with dark circles under his eyes. But he didn't get as grouchy with Ugly and me as he has been. He politely asked me to put Ugly outside for a while, so I did.

When I came back inside, Dad admitted that lately he might have been "overreacting to Ugly's excessive high spirits." He said that he won't chain or pen Ugly up, but he expects me to keep Ugly busy enough to be tired out at night. At the very moment Dad had finished saying this, Ugly started howling.

"He wants to be inside with us," I explained to Dad.

Dad looked up to the ceiling and took a deep breath. I think he was counting to ten. Dad always sticks to his word. I now know Ugly won't be locked or chained up. But I also know that Dad will keep on finding Ugly very annoying at times.

Whatever has happened to that rabbit, Ugly is out of a job again. Ugly and I have come to the very end of our list of possible dog careers. What would Sir Winston Churchill say now? You can tell people not to ever give up, but what if you completely run out of ideas? What then?

Ugly is coping with the disappointment better than I am. He's getting on with what matters most—loving his family. He is so excited when I come home from school each day that he still says "huuwoo" to me—the way I've taught him. He sleeps next to my bed. He's always thankful when I take him for his walks, groom, and feed him. He tries to be obedient for Grandpa, Dad, Mom, and me. He's patient with my sister, Gretchen, and he's polite to visitors.

But it doesn't help when my family's friends call or visit. They keep asking if Ugly has another job yet. In fact, since Ugly has helped to find the lost dog, Charlie McCaw, the whole neighborhood knows that Ugly wants a career.

When I walked past Mrs. Manchester's house today, she was sitting in her usual place on her veranda in the afternoon sunshine. She called out, "What job has Ugly got today?"

"He's taking a break, Mrs. Manchester," I said, trying not to sound annoyed.

Tonight, I decided that from now on, I'll tell people Ugly is on sabbatical. Grandpa explained that when people have been working hard for ages and ages, they are allowed to go on this very long holiday—maybe even for months. Just the same, Ugly going on long service leave seems like a sad ending to my book about Ugly getting a job. He's too young not to have a career.

I don't believe a book should end sadly. I like to

finish reading a book feeling all cheered up—enough
to keep my spirits high for a few days. I find it easier
to be nice to people when I'm cheerful. I don't want
anyone who reads this book to feel all heavy in the
heart because of its upsetting ending. I think I will
have to shove what I've written away and never show
anyone, not even Miss Jolly.

28

ere I am only a day later, writing as fast as my pen can write. Today surprised me more than I can ever say. It didn't seem like a day that would be surprising.

This morning, I didn't want to go to school. When I woke up, it was pouring down with rain. I tried all sorts of excuses with Mom like, "I think I might have a temperature" and "My foot hurts. I won't be able to walk around at school." When those excuses didn't work, I said, "Mom, you've got a vacation day from work today; why can't I have one too?"

Actually, I really was feeling tired, and I do have a cold. Mom eventually said, "How about I pick you up from school to save you walking?" We shook hands and made a deal.

●●●

The day felt extra long. It was one of those days when you keep looking at the clock, hoping the time will go faster. At lunchtime, the principal said all classes should stay inside because it was still raining heavily.

We might have been dry, but the shouting of tons of kids caged inside for an hour was awful. Barnaby put his hands over his ears and made a wailing noise. Miss Jolly let him choose a friend to spend time with for the rest of lunch in the office reception room. Barnaby chose me.

The reception room is for the principal to have meetings and chat with parents. It has a sofa, armchairs, and a coffee table. There are lamps (instead of bright lights) and even a little fridge so you can get cold drinks. The teacher's aide gave Barnaby some drawing paper and pencils, then she waited until Barnaby had settled down. She told us we could play quietly while she sat outside the open door.

"Draw us another Ugly picture," I said to Barnaby. He chose a pencil and started sketching. I saw Ugly running, his nose down on the ground. Then Barnaby drew a line of three ducks in front of Ugly. The duck at the front was flapping up into the air. I could almost hear it quacking angrily. Next, Barnaby drew me holding a pen and clipboard, looking as if I was trying to write down clever ideas for a dog job. I could tell it was me because I was a little bit plump and Ugly was looking at me in an excited way. He was holding a dog leash in his mouth as if to say, "I'm going to teach other dogs how to be obedient!"

After that, Barnaby drew Ugly leaping into the air, a USB stick flying toward his open mouth.

It amazed me that Barnaby knew so much about what's been happening with Ugly this year. He must have been listening to conversations I had with my friends when I thought he was not noticing anything. But it was Barnaby's drawings that totally stunned me.

"Can you show me how to draw a dog?" I asked Barnaby. "One like Ugly?"

Barnaby laughed excitedly and started drawing. I did my best to copy the way he made dog eyes seem lively and the way he could make a dog look like it was moving. By the time the bell rang for the end of lunch, I had covered a page with sketches.

"Thanks a bunch for the dog-drawing lessons, Barnaby," I said as we were walking back to class. "I'm starting to get the hang of it."

Once Miss Jolly had dismissed us at the end of the school day, I bolted out of the classroom, heading for the parents' parking lot. Milly and Hugh were still packing their bags, but Barnaby was just as excited as me to get home.

"I'll race you to the parking lot," I said. Barnaby

laughed. We started running. When we came to some puddles, we jumped into them, seeing who could make the biggest splash.

As we reached the parking lot, I noticed that Mrs. Fitzpatrick, Barnaby's mother, was standing next to Mom's car. Mom had her window down. The two mothers were chatting to each other. My heart leaped when I spotted Ugly sitting on the back seat of our car. Mom had wound his window down for him. He had his great big head and chest leaning out, eyes peering around, ears pricked up. I could tell he was looking for me.

"Hello there, Eric and Barnaby," said Mrs. Fitzpatrick, smiling at us as we reached the car.

"Hi, Mrs. Fitzpatrick," I said.

"Hop in, Eccle!" called Mom.

"Huuwoo!" Ugly said to me.

I opened the back door and was swinging my bag onto the seat when Barnaby cried out, "Ugwee! Ugwee!"

Ugly leaped out of the car in one gigantic bound and ran to Barnaby.

"Ugwee! Ugwee!" cried Barnaby again. He hugged Ugly tightly round the neck. Ugly wagged his tail and licked Barnaby's face. Barnaby laughed.

By now, my mom had jumped out of the car. Barnaby's mother looked terrified. She tried to pull Barnaby away. That was about as difficult as getting an oyster off a rock. Still hanging onto Ugly, Barnaby looked up at his mother. "Mom! Ugwee likes me!"

Barnaby's mother started to cry. My mom looked totally confused. But I understood. Barnaby's mother had just heard something she thought she'd never hear.

"Barnaby's speaking! Barnaby's speaking!" she said over and over again. At nine years old, her son had spoken his first sentence in public. I started to explain to Mom, but Barnaby's mother said to her, "This is a miracle. For years we've been hoping for a breakthrough. Barnaby's speech pathologist has been working so hard with Barnaby; she told us there might be a trigger to spark him off. She was right. It's Eric's dog, Ugly. Please would you and Eric let Barnaby have some time a few days each week with Ugly? I've heard schools sometimes even let special dogs keep children company!"

Mom asked, "What about it, Eccle?"

What did I think? Me sharing Ugly with Barnaby? At the start of this school year, I never thought I would feel the way I do now. But the fact is, at the moment I was—and still am—over the moon. At last my dog has a really, really important job. He is going to be a Barnaby helper!

I watched Ugly. He had now sat down, his back straight, his paws planted in front. He was huge and so very calm, like the king of all dogs. And he was still patiently letting Barnaby hug him. After a while, Barnaby relaxed, squeezing Ugly less tightly, just pressing his face into Ugly's furry neck and then leaning his cheek against Ugly's big-hearted chest.

"Ugly can spend time with Barnaby every single day, if you like," I said.

Barnaby's mother was so excited that the words tumbled out. "Thank you, Eric, thank you. Ugly will be the world's best companion dog for our Barnaby. Oh my goodness. To hear him speak in front of other people! I can't believe my ears!"

"I can tell Ugly loves you, Barnaby," I said to him. "It was time you two met."

Ugly gave Barnaby another sandpapery lick.

"I love Ugwee," cried Barnaby. "Lots!"

NOW THAT'S A HAPPY ENDING!

SQUEEZE!

WAG WAG

Acknowledgments

Special thanks to those people who have shared true stories about quirky things their dogs have done: the rescue dog, Oliver, whose dietary indiscretions are legendary in our family, and my Shepherd dog, Maud, who herded a dozen ducks into my bedroom.

To the children who thought up marvelous ideas for dog jobs, the young people who were happy to have a cameo role in the story, my Kiwi cousins who helped to fill in the plot hole that was as big and problematic as the hole Ugly made in Grandpa's rhubarb patch, and Anne Glass and Judy Valentine for their insights and creative suggestions.

A heartfelt thank-you is due to Jackie Pinkster and Gwendolen de Lacy, who possess both literary talent as well as understanding of the autism spectrum and who have generously offered frank and invaluable advice.

This story has been made immensely better due to

the editorial expertise of Jody Lee and the extremely close and careful scrutiny given to it by my structural editor, Kristy Bushnell. I am deeply thankful for this. Finally, I owe a debt of gratitude to my publisher, Kristina Schulz, who has always championed me in my journey as a writer.

About the Author

Elizabeth Fensham's first novel, *Helicopter Man*, won the 2006 CBCA Book of the Year for Younger Readers. It was followed by her young adult novels, *Miss McAllister's Ghost*, a 2009 CBCA Notable Book for Older Readers, *Goodbye Jamie Boyd*, shortlisted for the 2009 Bologna Book Fair's White Ravens Award, and *The Invisible Hero*, winner of the 2012 Speech Pathology Book of the Year Award and listed as an IBBY book. Elizabeth's younger reader novels include *Matty Forever*, shortlisted for the 2009 CBCA Book of the Year for Younger Readers, and the companions *Bill Rules*, shortlisted for the 2011 Queensland Premier's Literary Awards, and *Matty and Bill for Keeps*. The first of the My Dog Ugly series, *My Dog Made Me Write This Book*, was originally published in 2014. Elizabeth lives in Victoria's Dandenong Ranges.